"This is an intriguing, bold tale of mystery and faith, based on the ancient struggle between good and evil, right and wrong. Woven among family, friends and business relationships, and battles with the dark side of life, is the persistent strain of trying to do the right thing. I highly recommend this interesting piece of work."

> — Dr. Joe Martin, President and CAO of Atlanta Bible College and Church of God General Conference

"Author Robert Kmiecik demonstrates the narrative skills of a master novelist as he populates his complex and engaging story with memorable characters. A thoroughly entertaining read from beginning to end, "Saved...For Now" is highly recommended and will prove to be an enduringly popular addition to community library fiction collections.

> — *Midwest Book Review*, March, 2014

SAVED...
for now

SAVED...
for now

ROBERT KMIECIK

BlueJay House
Publishing LLC

OMAHA, NE

BlueJay House Publishing books may be ordered from your favorite bookseller, or purchased through Amazon.com and www.BlueJayHousePublishing.com.

Scripture taken from the HOLY BIBLE, NEW INTERNATIONAL VERSION ©. Copyright © 1973, 1978, 1984 by International Bible Society.

"NIV" and "New International Version" are trademarks registered in the United States Patent and Trademark office by International Bible Society.

BlueJay House Publishing
c/o CMI
13518 L. Street
Omaha, NE 68137

Paperback ISBN: 978-0-9913689-1-4
ePub ISBN: 978-0-9913689-3-8
Kindle ISBN: 978-0-9913689-2-1

Library of Congress Control Number: 2013958420

Certain stock imagery © iStockphoto

Designed and produced by Concierge Marketing Publishing Services.
Printed in the USA

10 9 8 7 6 5 4 3 2

INTRODUCTION

The heart of this story lies in the battle between right and wrong. Doing the right thing, or at least trying to; good versus evil; trying to live a life on the right side of a decision; staying on the path. But it is also a love story: God's. His love for every one of us and His hope that we make it.

The demarcation lines between right and wrong, good and evil, and even love and hate are not only blurred, but they move. They blur and zigzag moving almost randomly and differently for each of us. For the most part, the lines move subtly over time, not unlike the flow of a river whose channel is adjusted by floods or, more likely, by man. The Missouri river is the dividing boundary line for the states of Iowa and Nebraska, but its shores move over time. There is no clear boundary separating the two, but that's Mother Nature and is understandable.

But why do the lines between right and wrong, good and evil, love and hate move for us? Because we want them to. Or at least our minds conveniently allow them to.

The hundreds of decisions we make every day are influenced by many external forces like circumstances and people. Some of these influences come from a darker side, others from the light. The choices we make each day often flicker back and forth, on and off, right and wrong.

Just like in life, you will need to stop at times and think while reading this book. Take your time and read between the lines. Not every choice, decision, or action is clear, and it is up to you to determine what is right or wrong.

Like most books, this one is not for everyone. In fact, the readership may be low and some will shun its content and give up. However, the book was not written to sell thousands of copies, or even make a dime. But, if just one person, one reader, accepts its message, accepts Jesus in their heart and keeps Him there to the end, and is saved, not just for now, but forever, this book will be a success.

PROLOGUE

The meeting began at precisely 8:30 a.m. in the Dungeon, the large dark conference room in the basement of the downtown Atlanta branch of the Heller Federal Bank Building. Natas, the CEO of the Dark Angels, was last to enter and dimmed the lights even further. There were no windows, no way to see in or out—an intentional setting. A projector's fan was humming, but its light was off. The Sin Council, the Board of Directors for the Dark Angels, consisted of Natas and four team leaders all with a common purpose—to lead people to sin. They met every Monday morning, and whenever else he called them to report on their progress. Not unlike most businesses, they had goals, budgets, deadlines, incentives, and bills to pay. But they did not make any products or sell any useful services. No, they, and their many subordinates made people's lives miserable and tried to get them to sell their souls. Being members of the Sin Council meant that they had become the elite of the very worst.

Natas did not sit at the round table but had his own chair in the corner, barely visible.

"Let's hear from Lived first," he commanded.

"Yes, sir. Our team had a good week." Lived clicked on the projector light and showed a picture of a handsome young man. He could have modeled in fancy fragrance ads in men's magazines with his intoxicatingly good looks, dark brown hair, a thin but firm build, smooth tan skin, and inviting eyes of sapphire.

"You might remember Christian. He joined us part-time a couple months ago and was at our last quarterly forum."

"Yes, the kid's adorable," said Natas from the corner. "How's he doing? Is he up to no good?"

"His main project involves Victoria Wander and he's very excited about it." Lived clicked his mouse and a lovely lady appeared innocently on the screen.

"She is forty, married with two small kids being raised by a nanny. Her husband travels a lot. She works way too many hours, just two cubicles across from Christian at Coca-Cola. She is training him to take over as one of the company's accounts receivable clerks. Her goal is to become CFO. His assignment is to seduce her."

"And?"

"He has been giving her his attention and compliments her work and dress. She finally agreed to go to lunch with him today." A rare smile appeared from the corner of the room.

"Nice. Why don't you suggest that he give her a small gift, just a token of his appreciation for her training, of course."

"Yes, sir, good idea. May I advance him some seed money?"

"Of course, and give Christian the resources he needs to secure the seduction. By the way, team leaders, I am meeting with the finance department after our meeting, and my advance report sounds promising. Our drug rings and brothels are doing well, most pleasing to our leader. I may be able to increase your budgets." The drug and prostitution rings they ran bankrolled Natas and his Sin Council's syndication of sin to satisfy Satan.

"Lived, what about that father-daughter pastor duo you've been working on?"

Lived clicked off the projector and the room became darker than before. Natas increased the light wattage a little. He controlled the lights, and about everything else, on those rare occasions when Satan so empowered him. Satan could reach out and touch Natas to give him surreal powers, but his success working through the Sin Council and their teams on Earth made it unnecessary most of the time. A cold stillness hovered over them as Lived paused for a few seconds. He fiddled with some papers, seemingly buying time, and then continued in the grayness. He did not like conveying bad news, and knew that his boss hated hearing it even more.

"They have been most difficult, as expected. The father is retiring so he won't be saving many souls anyway. He is stubbornly holy and resists all of our temptations. We made him late for an appointment once, and he would not even break the speed limit. He slaps away our sin shots like a great hockey goalie. The man is a devout Christian. I suggest we let him retire and focus our resources elsewhere."

"Agreed. What about the daughter?" Natas's concurrence gave Lived a sense of relief though he could still feel the tension in the room. The other three leaders had said not a word or hardly moved a muscle since he sat in the corner. Lived continued.

"Likewise, she is a hard nut to crack. She is passionate in her ministry and is a threat to our cause. We have tried to weaken her resolve through poor health for her as well as her son. As you know, we have our ways. We've also tried to spread some gossip and infighting at the church, but she squelches it and steadfastly stays strong and squarely on the path. And, to make matters worse, we are having difficulty raising sin with many of her friends and followers as well, as she has successfully shared her religious bent with others. She is keeping others on the path, too."

"She is a problem, indeed. Let's become really blunt with her. Make her aware of our real presence and capabilities, and threaten her eleven-year-old son if she will not stop her ministry," the corner commanded.

"Will do. I have an associate in mind to assign," Lived went on. "I wanted also to introduce a new project. Last week you suggested that as part of our focus on religious leaders that we take a look at some young pastors and try to 'nip 'em in the bud' I believe were your words, sir. My team has identified a twenty-two-year-old recent graduate from the local Bible College whose future as a pastor looks way too promising. He already has an impressive following. He graduated at the top of his class, had several pastoral job offers, speaks Latin and Hebrew, can quote Scripture like the Pope, and lives a humble life. His presence and message seem to attract people. Our analysts have crunched some numbers, and he is clearly our biggest young rival. I want to follow him, uh, I mean keep track of him."

"Yes, Lived. Good work in identifying our target. I want him on our agenda each week going forward. In fact, let's put you, and him, at the top of the agenda until further notice."

Lived concluded his report on a few more projects and, one by one, the Sin Council went around the table and gave updates on their progress of ruining and destroying lives with the help of some synthetic sin.

†

Jakson Andru Ross had just graduated with the highest honors and distinction from the prestigious Atlanta Bible College, and at the tender age of twenty-two was a licensed pastor. He had been called to the ministry at a very young age and was already one of the best. No one, except his God, actually knew his potential and how good Jak was and would be at his calling. As part of his studies he had already practiced his preaching to people in a plethora of places on the planet. He had preached as an intern in places between the heart of the United States and the horn of Africa. Despite his youth, or maybe because of it, his theological knowledge and ministerial talents came coupled with compassion and a proven track record. Even in a tough job market with church attendance declining in the United States, he had several offers from many churches. But the local church where he had interned was not going to let him get away.

Due to extenuating circumstances, the Eternal Life Church of God had recently hired him as their head pastor, and immediately knew they were blessed with a very special young man. He was attracting followers and saving souls. One of his church's elders used the analogy that if Jak was a college football player he would have been the number one overall pick in the NFL draft. The elder felt that the Eternal Life Church of God hit the lottery in the draft.

But Jak's uncanny God-given ability to steer people away from sin and toward Jesus had also made him the number one target of the devil's team on Earth. Natas and his Sin Council of the Dark Angels had become hell-bent on stopping Pastor Jak Ross before he even got started and were determined to stop him from saving souls.

Jak was in trouble. Big trouble.

1

Natas entered the Dungeon late for the meeting and immediately ordered the Sin Council to disarm all electronic devices. He closed the door and sealed its edges, and once seated in his corner, eliminated what little light was left. The five present could not see their hands before their faces, let alone anyone or anything else. Just what he wanted. The room was pure darkness, like the blackness you see in the deep bowels of the darkest cave when the guide extinguishes all light. Just as chilled as well.

"Do you see what I see? You may see nothing, but from my corner, I see everything. Today, I want your reports without the accompaniment of notes, computers, gestures, and expressions. Email me your complete updates after our meeting, but for now I only want to hear what you have to say."

Lived's report on Jak Ross troubled Natas, and Lived could sense evil unrest in the corner. According to Lived, the young pastor's church was thriving with Sunday attendance up 70 percent since he started just a few weeks earlier, and he was averaging over four baptisms a week. His Youth Group and Sunday School numbers were also growing more than the average in their database, and more impressive (though very concerning to Natas), the attendance rate among active members was over 90 percent, compared to the average church rate of 47 percent. Lived explained further, "In other words, his followers are not only growing in number, they are also growing in commitment and resolve to attend each week. For the first time ever at this church, a majority of his followers want a midweek mass."

"Our soft attempts to sway Ross off the path have had little impact. He disdains porn, throws away our free coupons to our adult bookstore, waved off our palm reader offers, and turned our drug sample over to the police. We tried to engage him in gossip and he instead gave our associate on-the-spot counseling, and a summation on the danger and unhealthiness of gossipy rumor, and turned the conversation into Gospel. His followers are also less receptive to our sin attractants than we normally experience. We have tried..."

"I've heard enough," the corner interrupted abruptly. "I'm going to call on the boy personally. He's a big problem long term. Move on. Next topic."

On a more positive note, Lived went on in the darkness to report that Christian Wright's efforts to seduce Victoria Wander were advancing nicely, and a formal secret "date" had been scheduled. The nanny could cover the kids and work would draw Wander's husband away.

But the best news may have been his update on the father-daughter pastoral team that had agreed to surrender their calling. Since they quit a few weeks earlier, they had not saved a single new soul. Lived concluded his report with mixed results.

The Dungeon was still pitch black.

Sinbad then gave a quick update on the blast text message campaign. They were starting a project of sending out texts such as "OMG. I cud c whr this was goin" during rush hour traffic that would look like it was sent by someone the recipient knew. The objective was to distract drivers to destruction or death. Based on how they got their phone numbers and the data available, *these people* thought their recipients were unsaved. They could care less if the recipients crashed into others.

They called it "Project Never Mind".

Other members of the Sin Council gave their verbal reports in the darkness on planting seeds of sin, nurturing ruined lives, and harvesting heartache and hardship.

When Natas abruptly turned on the light and fled his corner sporting red shades, they were all blinded.

Thursday, March 20

It may have been the calm before the storm.

I was relaxing comfortably downstairs, no longer Rob Ross the attorney, but Rob Ross the couch potato. Even so, I could faintly hear the thunder rumble several seconds after the distant lightning flashed through the basement windows. It was early spring in Nebraska, and the winter had been mild and dry so we needed the rain. But sometimes these innocent spring showers can be accompanied by destructive tornadoes, hail, and high winds destroying both property and lives.

I always had a fear of the storm *after* the calm, not just for the weather, but for life as well. If you're lucky, once in a while things can just seem to go your way. It can be little things, such as a break at work, your adversaries make missteps, you hit mostly green lights, your investments are up this year, or you simply stay healthy. It can also be the absence of negative things, like the lack of a bad work review, no flat tire, no misbehaving children, no sickness, or other annoyances. The positive things in our lives and/ or the lack of negative ones can cumulatively result in calm seas for smooth sailing, as things seem to go your way. But this calm can be dangerous, misleading, and give a false sense of security.

Things seemed to be going fairly well, both at work and at home. At work, things at the law firm were still going great, and the future looked as bright as the past. I was hitting a pretty good percentage of my hunches and educated guesses, and my clients were happy. At home, everyone was healthy, staying out of trouble, had Jesus in their hearts, and Sheryl and the kids were all doing well and seemed to know where they were destined.

I had a productive day at work helping clients and going through the daily grind. I prefer calm routines and really do not like surprises, especially bad ones. A good day is when everything goes as planned, and the proverbial 'been there done that' permeates most activities. As surely as the sun rises and sets, so could many of us rise and set contently in our ways. I prefer habits and routines, things I can do without much thought, so I can save brain power for more strategic issues. Kind of like life on cruise control.

On this particular night I was finally downstairs in my man cave relaxing with two of my best friends, Teddy and Itty Bitty. We've always had dogs and, of course, allow ourselves to get emotionally attached to someone, some*thing*, that really does not live that long. The attachment eventually ends and causes household sadness every few years. In fact, we just recently had to put one of my good friends, Daisy, to sleep. Maybe that is why we've always had two or three dogs—to make sure we never have none. In our view, a house without a dog or two is just not a home. Oh, how the world would be so much better if more people were more like a gentle, subservient dog—loyal, genuinely loving, happy to see you, and you them. If people had tails, I would hope they would wag often.

My little canine friends were with me on the couch watching March Madness. It was the second weekend of the NCAA basketball tournament, and Brigham Young University was playing without one of their best players. He had apparently violated one of the school's codes of conduct—premarital sex. After having heard this, I had to look up the school's code of conduct on the Internet to see how I would fare under such a code, and after getting depressed, I stopped. Their code is quite stringent. Especially at the loss of the player, BYU was clearly an underdog as we watched these religious, clean-cut, mostly Caucasian, tattoo-less overachievers take on a major conference power, Cincinnati. The Cincy Bearcats were huge and athletic and treated their bodies like canvases to be painted with broad needle strokes. They had also had their share of scandals, brawls, and NCAA probations through the years. Not only was it easy to root for BYU, the underdog in a David versus Goliath match, but this match-up also had a pinch of good versus evil.

Lightning was followed more closely by thunder. The storm was approaching. Sometimes we can see or sense it coming, and sometimes it blows in unexpectedly.

Sheryl was coming down the stairs. Mrs. Calm. One of her attractants to me. I knew it was Sheryl because of experience. After living in this house for more than twenty-seven years, I could tell not only when someone was coming down the stairs, but who amongst our family it was. The steps are original and wooden with open space between them and make sounds as unique as the people descending. Sheryl has a methodical approach, the same speed every time she makes the descent—consistent perhaps with her carefree but determined stay-at-home-mom personality. We recently celebrated our twenty-seventh anniversary and she walks those stairs today the same way she did the first day. And always still, the same consistent speed. Uncompromising and steady when faced with right or wrong. Another attractant. I guess opposites attract.

I could tell when our oldest was coming down the stairs because he was usually whistling, snapping his fingers, humming, or even singing and grinning. Almost always grinning. That would be our twenty-two-year-old adopted son, Jak, who just graduated from Bible College as a pastor and started leading a church down in Georgia. He had found his calling at a young age, and somehow it showed in his gait down these stairs. Confident, carefree, but caring about others, and knowing where he was going now and forever. And he was determined to take as many people with him as he could. His ability to capture followers had escaped me at first.

Our second oldest, Jakob, was a little more difficult to detect when he came downstairs. He's like a lot of us. He usually took the longest to make his way down the steps, as if he was thinking different thoughts with each one. Sometimes he'd just stop on a step for a few seconds thinking, texting, whatever. I can always tell when Jakob is coming downstairs, but I still struggle to know what is going on between his ears. I think it is mostly good, but he is guarded in what he shares. He is on an academic scholarship finishing his junior year at Creighton University in their pre-med program, as he wants to be a doctor. I guess Jakob will help mend people's bodies for a few years, whereas Jak will be saving people's souls forever. Jakob is also our jokester. My secretary, Eileen, is close to our family and often bakes us cinnamon rolls. The *best* cinnamon rolls! Once I had the kids write her a thank-you note. Jakob wrote her that the rolls were "sooo good that I had to beat up J-Rod for the last one." Eileen still has that thank-you note to this day.

I knew when J-Rod, as we affectionately call him, was coming downstairs because he'd either be finishing up a conversation upstairs with Mom after he could no longer see her, or beginning one downstairs with me before he could see me. If he wasn't doing that, I could tell it was him because his big frame made just a little bit louder thump on each step. He had outgrown his older brothers, and now he gets as many of Eileen's rolls as he wants.

It's funny how brothers become more diplomatic and less physical with their disagreements as the younger ones catch or surpass the elder ones in size and strength. Or maybe they just mature. But J-Rod is so thoughtful and caring about others. Ever since he was old enough to care, he has cared so much about others. Believe me; he did not get all that from me. I remember one time the boys and I were playing basketball in our concrete driveway.

The games sometimes were intense and competitive. As I became the fourth best player among us, J-Rod had become the best. So he and I would take on Jak and Jakob, numbers two and three. A loose ball was bouncing out of bounds, and J-Rod and Jak got tangled up trying to save it. J-Rod slipped backwards and fell to the pavement. He has a scar on his forearm now, but the more serious injury occurred when his head hit the pavement. It sounded horrific, and a million bad thoughts went through my mind as I rushed to his side. He was bleeding and his eyes rolled up under his lids. He was convulsing and in shock. I put my arm under his head and felt a knot had already swelled up. He briefly came to and he said, "Dad, whose ball is it?" He then looked dazed and still in shock, but we were able to get him to his feet with our assistance. Sheryl and I were driving him to the ER when he said we need to call Jak. Why? He wanted us to tell Jak that he knew it was not Jak's fault and it was just an accident. J-Rod ended up recovering just fine—other than that scar he still sports. I would not be surprised if J-Rod also joined the ministry, or another profession serving others. He is a freshman at St. Joseph's University on a basketball scholarship and is coming home next week on spring break. I can't wait.

The easiest person in our family that I can detect coming downstairs is our youngest, our only daughter, J'Nay. We adopted J'Nay from Korea, and I often kid with her that she is my favorite daughter. She practically flies down those stairs. Ever since she could walk, she would always run up and down the stairs. After pleading with her the first hundred times or so to slow down so as not to hurt herself, I gave up. She is now a sophomore in high school and to this day, every time she comes down those steps she's in a big hurry. For what, I've never known. She wanted to go on a mission trip with the boys but we thought she was a little too young. She was always trying to keep up with her older brothers, and in some ways, surpassed them. Her choices were good for the most part, and I am very proud of my favorite daughter.

Sometimes I wish genes flowed upstream. All of our kids try to serve others. They are young and make the same mistakes as their peers and succumb to their pressure, but they also love and serve others. I remember not long ago when all three boys were on mission trips and I sent this email out to some of my friends and family:

> Just wanted to let you know that Jak just landed in Nairobi to start a month-long mission trip in Africa. He will help build churches and distribute Bibles and Gospel in three African countries. He rests and stays at a palace for two days then goes into the poverty-stricken areas. He will help share the Word to many who are hungry for it. In Africa they can build a brand-new church for two thousand dollars and can feed one person for a whole year for fifty dollars. Jak is disconnected from us for the most part, as cell service is severed.

†

> J-Rod and Jakob are in Haiti on a mission trip. They have been there since Sunday and will return this Sunday. It is perhaps the poorest people-populated place on the planet. From the Port-au-Prince airport they rode in the back of a truck for three hours on dirt roads to the orphanage and "medical clinic" where they will serve. Their first meal was goat. They had milk preserved from the same goat. We've seen

photos of them playing with very skinny kids, but with rare smiles on their faces. I suspect it will be hard for the boys to say good-bye and leave the kids to survive in a world without much hope. They will come home with virtually empty baggage, as they intend to give away all their clothes, personal effects, and anything not needed for the trip back.

Please take a second to keep these guys in your prayers, to serve well those they meet with, and to come home safe, changed for the better forever.

Thank you,
Rob

Sometimes, great kids can shame even good parents.

As Teddy is curling up to me on the comfortable man cave couch I realized that my love for him reminds me of God's love for us. Teddy is the dumb, undeserving, long-haired male dachshund with black hair and brown socks. I can't tell when he is coming down the stairs because he can't come down the stairs. Actually, he probably can, but he's just so much of a little baby he won't come down the stairs. He will whine from up on the landing wanting to join us, and I have to go up and bring him down to the man cave, and then when it is time to go up, we have to carry him up. Maybe he does not navigate the stairs because we have always helped him up and down. When we go outside, he doesn't even lift his leg, he just squats like the wiener dog that he is. Good grief. We even have a fire hydrant in our front yard that he has never lifted on. Once I carry him down here, he will saunter around looking for food the kids or I may have dropped or abandoned. In some ways, he reminds me of Templeton, the rat in E.B. White's *Charlotte's Web*. Sometimes he has an "accident" down here. How dare he go in the man cave? He can be a pretty pathetic pet, but right now he is cuddling up to my lap and is placing his snout on my leg. He glances up at me as if to say "thank you, Dad," closes his eyes, exhales, and totally relaxes. After a quick pet I rest my hand on his soft plush neck and think to myself, "Gosh, I love this dog."

Bitty, on the other hand, navigates those steps as well as anyone. The little gray ball of fur also runs up and down them. Why? She likes it in the man cave, too, especially when I am down here. I share my snacks and my love with her. Bitty is easy to love and welcomes any and all into our home with a wagging tail. She has one speed—fast. Like J'Nay—maybe it's something about the young females in the house that like to run up and down the stairs.

But this time, the person coming down the steps was clearly Sheryl. She reached the bottom and turned into the man cave.

"Who's winning?" We had met at Creighton and she was a big college basketball fan as well.

Before I could answer, she looked at the big screen and said, "Rats." She, too, knew that the game was a David versus Goliath match, good versus bad on some levels, and Cincinnati was killing the underdog BYU by twenty points midway through the second half.

Why do we root for the underdog? Partly because many of us are underdogs ourselves, often overcoming ominous odds.

"The storm's getting closer," she said.

"Yeah, the thunder is only a few seconds behind the lightning flashes now, about one mile away."

"I think I am going to turn in for the night," she said. "But if the sirens go off J'Nay and I will be down to join you."

"Sounds good, g'night, but don't forget Ted. I mean to bring him down too if the sirens go off." She took Teddy and ascended the stairs. Bitty always waited for me, probably because we usually shared a bedtime snack, like chips or other junk.

I decided to mute the TV and say my nightly prayer. The wind was really howling and the storm approaching.

I thought to myself, though life seems calm and smooth sometimes, we live in a world of storms. Some are huge, like hurricanes, while other weather conditions are small and result in little or no damage.

There are also storms in our personal lives—some big, some small. But throughout them all we need to remember is that God loves us. So much that He allowed His only Son to die for us, to suffer through a horrible "storm" on Earth in order to save us from sin and death, but only if we accept and hold Jesus in our hearts and walk with him as our Savior. Storms in this life can be devastating and horrible. But for those who do not have Jesus in their hearts, the storms in the next life will be far worse.

I finished my prayer and unmuted the TV before I powered it off. This time I remembered. Maybe the storm and circumstances kept my senses straight. BYU had lost, but it was just a game.

The rain had begun and the thunder and lightning were a little louder and brighter. The lightning and thunder were now simultaneous, but this storm would only bring much needed moisture. No twisters, hail, or high winds. The storm quickly passed this time, and the calm was back, for now. I was about to go upstairs with Bitty right behind me, both of us bound for bed.

Little did I know, the day-to-day calmness, the slow grinding routine that I and so many other people prefer, was about to come to an end.

2

I don't get many calls on my cell phone. I know this is contrary to most folks these days, and I get even less on our home's land line, which is fine with me. Most of my incoming calls are at work—too many actually. I usually don't even have my cell on me and I leave it in my truck or car. I don't like incoming calls, and I ignore most on my cell. Gotta love Caller ID. No wonder I don't get that many calls, and that is fine with me. Although, I wish I could tell when God was trying to call or talk to me.

Anyway, for whatever reason, I had my iPhone on me, so I could at least check work emails—not necessarily reply. I hate the warp-speed pace of technology these days, it makes me feel like the pace car in a NASCAR race when it goes from caution to green. Remember, I think the calm routine is good. Fifty-five miles per hour is fast enough. Constant connection to an ever-changing and dangerous world is not always good, especially if done carelessly or addictively.

Bark bark, I had the ring tone set up to sound like a barking dog. I guess some technology is okay. Bitty perked up but realized it was just my phone and curled back into her nest on the couch. I was a bit taken aback when the incoming number showed up. Jak? He only called if he needed something. So why was this rare call coming in? He was much closer to his mom, and he usually called her first to chat, and then she would give me the phone. So why call me? Good question, so I answered.

"Daddy, it's Jak." Good grief, I knew the voice of our oldest son, and when he did call, he usually did not feel the need to identify himself. But his voice *was* a little different.

"Hi, how's it going so far? Going great down there?" I asked. Our oldest, at twenty-two, had just become a pastor and moved south near Atlanta to join a church with his young bride, and I was sure he'd be next to Jesus Christ on cloud nine or something. Not exactly.

"Dad, can *you* come see us?" he asked, with the most subdued, troubled, confused tone I had ever heard from our otherwise happy-go-lucky adopted son. I can usually sense when someone is in trouble, even on the phone without the assistance of body language or facial expressions. Twenty-seven years of practicing law and helping people solve problems has its advantages. Jak had seen me help numerous clients as well as friends and family resolve their problems. He sounded troubled, and he knew I was great at solving other peoples' problems. Sometimes I struggle with my own problems and could use someone like me to help me.

"Well, yeah, we'll come visit sometime soon," I said.

"Dad?" I clearly was now sensing something was not right.

"Yes," I replied with a little trepidation, not sure where this was going.

"Dad, you know I am totally all in with this Christian calling and I am going to save a *lot* of souls, right?"

In the old days, I would have thought, *yeah, right—you, Tim Tebow, and Joel Osteen will save the world.* But I did see the genuine calling grow in our son who had even drawn me closer to Jesus. I now believed he would indeed save many people, er, souls. Maybe, even miraculously, mine.

"I *know* you are, Jak, and you know I am totally on board with you. You have strengthened me in my faith, and I am all in with you."

Jak responded, "Yes, I know you know I am. That's why I called *you*. You're also very smart and can help people." After twenty or so years, Jak and I were finally seeing eye-to-eye. Well, not really.

Anyway, his next eye-to-eye with me blindsided me and really got my heart pumping.

"Dad, you're on your cell, right?"

"Yes, down here with Bit." I was still downstairs in the basement man cave with Itty Bitty, sharing some Doritos.

"Okay, Dad. Shelly and I have only been here a few weeks, but J-Rod warned us about *these people*, and he was right."

"Jak, you're kinda scaring me. What are you talking about *these people*?"

"J-Rod told Shelly and me to save as many souls as possible, but to be careful to make sure *these people* never prevent us from saving our own, and to never let them stop us from saving other souls."

"How does J-Rod know about *these people*?"

"He said they were studying groups like them in his theology class."

I thought about conferencing in J-Rod right then to ask him what he knew and how. But it was late, especially back east. Besides, J-Rod might say something Jak need not hear, and Jak might share something J-Rod did not need to know. I would follow up with J-Rod later.

"Okay."

"Well," Jak continued, "*These people* J-Rod warned us about are already trying to get me to stop my calling, and they mean business. I think I'm in trouble. They are threatening us if I don't stop."

"Who?"

"I'll explain when you get here. Dad, we need you here tomorrow."

I didn't like this at all. I had a lot of questions, but I knew Jak would not have the answers. Clearly, Jak needed me as soon as possible. He'd never asked for this type of urgent help before. I had to make a decision I had not had to ever make before, and it would not be my last.

"Mom and I are on our way," I assured Jak.

"No Dad, just you!"

Friday, March 21

Of course, I took the next flight out of Omaha to Atlanta on Friday morning. The flight was at 6:00 a.m. which meant I had to get up at 3:00 a.m. to get cleaned up, packed, and ready to get through the airport security hassles. I'm not the drop-everything type, but geez, Jak's voice and tone were very out of character. I knew he needed me now.

Sheryl knew me well enough to know that if I was unexpectedly going to Atlanta, especially without her, something must be wrong. I told her part of the reason I was going, but I did not know it all either. She was worried and wanted to go. She worried even more when I told her I wanted her here to safeguard J'Nay and the dogs. I could not agree to promise her the full updates she asked for when we said good-bye at 3:59 a.m.

I had partners at the law firm who would cover for me. In fact, a colleague in Atlanta had recently called to see if he could help me with anything. We had offices in several cities, and this Atlanta partner was an old criminal law attorney. At the time, I had no clue why he thought he needed to offer me his assistance. In his criminal law days, Stan Manilow had learned lots of tricks of the trade and street smarts, but again, not really anything I or my clients needed. I represented businesses and corporate clients, not criminals. He was tired of representing killers, rapists, druggies, and thieves, so he became an estate planning lawyer. He now helps people plan their estates for when they die and thereafter. Oddly, Stan mentioned that he had heard of a new pastor who had just graduated and settled at a church nearby who was fishing for souls. I knew it was Jak. Turns out, so did Stan. But at the time I still did not see the connection between Stan and Jak.

We landed in Atlanta, and even with no checked bags, getting through an airport terminal was a hassle. I found an ATM to get some cash, and there was a twenty-dollar bill someone had left behind in the money dispenser tray. I looked around, but there was no way I could tell who had lost or left it. I wondered what I should do. Later I asked Sheryl her opinion, and I should have thought of her response. She suggested I give it to the church.

After walking a short marathon, I stopped at the food court. They were busy, rude, and expensive. The clerk gave me coffee instead of tea, sausage instead of bacon, and royally screwed up my order with no cheese! Geez. I tried to let it go, but a bad taste lingered.

I knew the devil wanted me to just keep that twenty bucks I found, and to complain and be rude back to the clerk. We are in a constant duel with the devil every day. Sometimes we win, sometimes he does. We try to do the right thing, choose good over bad, but he tries to negatively influence our decisions. He basically attacks us in two ways: He tries to get us to do things we should not, and he tries to get us to not do things we should.

Very simple.

The devil tries to influence us in even the smallest decisions. Do we go faster than the speed limit? Do we gossip or partake in rumors? Cheat or lie? Do we skip a class at school or call-in sick at work when we are not? Do we roll with the punches and drive in traffic with courtesy and willingness to yield, or do we flip the occasional bird?

Of course, Satan also tries to steer us further off the path and convince us to do more serious wrongs, like repetitiously lie, cheat, steal, violate the Commandments, commit a crime, or hurt someone. As humans, we are going to sin, but Satan tries to make us repeat our mistakes.

Fortunately, if we listen closely enough we can also hear God talking to us.

I decided to find a seat right there in the terminal and go over my poem. I wrote a poem a while back when I sensed Satan trying to influence me, and I needed to hear God talking to me. I re-read my poem again, and again.

God Talked to Me Today

God talked to me today,
Maybe he spoke to me through someone;
perhaps it was you.
But God talked to me today; I know it's true.
He helped me realize there are some things in my life
I need to change,
Some relationships, priorities, some character traits
I need to rearrange.
God talked to me today.
He helped me see at times I wander astray,
Off the path on which we need to try to stay.
It's up to me. I know what I need to do.
God talked to me today.
Maybe, just maybe, he talked to you, too.

I finished my delicious coffee and sausage croissant-wich, forgave the rude clerks, and resolved to give the twenty dollars to the church. He did talk to me again. This time I listened.

Another long trek finally took me to the car rental, and I picked one up and headed to Jak and Shelly's.

After driving a few minutes, I sensed a tail so obvious he must have been an amateur. The same neon-green car had been following me closely since I left Hertz. Someone was following me. Unbelievable. I was just trying to help my son with a problem, and someone was following me! I did not know what to do, so I just kept driving. I took a couple unintended turns to confirm, and he was definitely following me.

I decided to take up the offer from Stan, who answered my cell call.

"Hello, Stan Manilow."

"Stan, its Rob Ross from our Omaha office."

"Great, I was about to call you. Where are you?"

"Well, I actually just landed in Atlanta. Why? And why call me?"

"I knew you were coming, but you're in trouble. Exactly where are you?"

"Why? What's up?"

"Where the hell are you, Ross?"

"Glad to talk to you, too, Stan. But, I just pulled off I-85 near Sullivan Road."

He was able to meet me, but he was fifteen minutes away. He directed me to this undeveloped residential area to buy some time. At the time, I thought I could not lead my tail to Jak and Shelly's, so I drove around a while but didn't really try to ditch them. It turned out that they knew where I was going then and perhaps forever. Damn technology. I reached the residential area without the residences. The economic downturn had stopped all construction, some in mid-stream. It was desolate, so I simply pulled over. Why? I figured I would just ask my tail what he wanted. I couldn't believe what he wanted. It happened so fast.

He wanted me. The tail parked behind me, and my backup, Stan, just arrived. He parked right behind the neon green and boxed him in. I decided to sit tight and watch through my mirrors. My tail stayed in his car as Stan headed toward the boxed-in car. Without hesitation, Stan approached the car, drew a pistol, and killed my tail. Holy crap! I was in a daze as I got out and went to the tail's car, and notwithstanding the tinted driver's window with a single bullet hole in it, I could clearly see he was dead. I heard that Stan was crazy, but he had just killed someone following me with the skill of a seasoned sniper. The single shot pierced straight through my tail's head.

"Stan, what the hell did you do that for?"

Showing little emotion, he yelled, "Ross, we gotta get outta here. Meet me at the office. I'll tell you more then."

"But why did you kill this man?"

"Because he knew I was coming, and if I didn't kill him now *you'd* be dead! Besides, I wanted to send *these people* a message."

"What? *These people?* How'd he know I arrived and that you were coming?"

"Rob, just keep in mind that *these people* are listening to all of your phone calls until I can get us some secure ones."

"*These people?*" I took another look at my dead tail. "But Stan, how did you know he was going to kill me? I mean, you did not even try to reason with him."

"We have an informant among them. When you called me, they were listening to you and knew I was coming. I'm surprised you survived, frankly. Our informant called me right after you did when I was on my way to meet you. She had an urgent update and said your tail was instructed to take you out without haste. If I had not come, or even hesitated, you would assuredly be dead."

"I can't believe this." Before I could say any more, he ran for his pickup.

"See you at the office, Ross. And hurry!"

Where the hell was this going?

3

This was getting serious in a hurry. I could not believe it—a life taken, a life saved. But then, life on Earth is short and its length is almost irrelevant in the long term. Life's substance is much more important than its length. I've always thought that if we are saved by accepting Jesus in our hearts, and we are promised forever in the Kingdom when we die, are the believers who die, especially those who die young, the lucky ones? But in the short term, existence can be very important. Thanks to Stan, I still had mine, at least according to him. My unlucky tail was killed, so I could now go to Jak and Shelly's, but I didn't know how many tails *these people* might have. I needed to let Jak know I was going to be late, probably closer to 2:00 p.m. I didn't care who may be listening so I dialed Jak's cell. "Hello…"

"Jak, it's Daddy."

Jak did not actually answer. His voicemail greeting is his voice saying *hello* so you think he answered, but then you are prompted to leave a message. So I did. I fall for it still. Its like he's there for you, even if he's not.

We hightailed it to the firm's office, and simply left my tail behind. We headed north toward downtown, and the sirens passed by going south to check out the dead tail. It was a short drive to the office. Stan was driving an average pickup that he parked in his garage stall, but I had to find a spot on the street outside. He beat me up to the twenty-seventh floor, the Atlanta office's main reception lobby, where I was greeted by Flo.

"Hey, welcome Mr. Robinson Ross, my favorite partner in our Omaha office." McGill Hecker spared no expense on office facilities or staff. Sweet Flo was very pretty and personable and dressed the part. Despite my morning so far, I was able to respond, "Thanks Flo, er, my favorite receptionist on the twenty-seventh floor."

"Nice one, Rob. Mr. Manilow had me set up the visiting attorney office for you. It's right there, with a sandwich and water waiting for you."

"And do I get an orange jumpsuit and one phone call, too?"

Flo giggled and said, "Stanley wants you to meet him in the Coliseum at 2:00 p.m."

The Coliseum was the firm's most secure, swept, de-bugged conference room, locked down, and reserved for clients who had to be sure what was spoken by them and their counsel remained secure and confidential. The attorney-client privilege on steroids.

"Why the Coliseum?" I asked.

"Rob, I just call 'em as I see 'em," said Flo at her best.

"Nice."

I proceeded to the visiting attorney billing station, er, office. It was elegant but functional. Cherry wood desk and credenza with glass tops. Stunning view of the Atlanta skyline, with numerous skyscrapers reaching for the heavens. Law firms try to project an intellectual image of legal brilliance, dedicated to the best interests of their clients, of course. The pursuit of justice in these legal factories churns out tons of paper and counsel, little more than widgets of perceived wisdom. Heck, half the time they just make educated guesses.

I had some calls to make before 2:00 p.m. Jak again first. *Hello...* I did not fall for it this time and left an updated message. Probably closer to 5:00 p.m. now before I could get to his place. Yesterday he implored that he needed me here tomorrow, today, I am here, and he isn't taking or returning my calls. Hmmm. Well, I could not be there quite yet anyway, but couldn't Jak at least call me back, leave me a message.

Next, I called Sheryl. Again, I had to leave a message.

I called my assistant in Omaha. "This is Eileen." I knew she would answer.

"Hey, it's Rob. How..."

"What are you doing in Atlanta?" she interrupted. Eileen is the absolutely dependable best, and almost always answers. I am pretty much in the office every day at 8:00 a.m. If I am going to be out or late, I advise Eileen. By 8:01 a.m. she was wondering about my whereabouts. I saw she had called my cell, but I did not call her back.

"How'd you know I was in Atlanta?"

"I called Sheryl. She said something had come up in Atlanta and you had taken a very early flight. So then I called Flo, and you were not in yet at 11:30 a.m. What were you doing?"

"I was already working my tail off."

"Okay, I handled your morning stuff, but Mr. Milo is coming in at 3:00 p.m. my time. I called and told him you might not be here, but he seemed fine meeting with just me."

"Great, Eileen. You'll do fine, but you can't practice law." Eileen was not a lawyer or even a paralegal, but she helped take care of my clients better than any partner of mine had in twenty-seven years of practice, and clients loved working with her. "You know it's illegal for you to practice law."

"I don't practice," she said. "I perfect it, if I can. And, I know you are just covering yourself, Rob."

She was right, but so was I.

Mr. Milo owned Schneider Distribution, the country's largest distributor of cattle semen. Cows don't do sex very well, so to make sure they keep producing and we have plenty of milk, burgers, and Omaha Steaks, most cows have to be artificially inseminated. How they get those bulls to create or produce the product Milo distributes, I should probably learn about someday. Know your client's business, right?

Milo's semen business is huge and growing. He was renewing a five-year contract with a large multi-state cattle operation with over one million head that were not getting any, and needed help reproducing. The contract with Custom Farms was worth more than five and a half million dollars per year, but with the price of beef low and the cost to feed and fatten those virgins high, Milo's large customer was struggling financially.

It was hard to concentrate, but even with *these people* wreaking havoc in our lives, business continued. Despite what trials and tribulations come our way, life has a persistent, annoying way of continuing on.

"Eileen, I read the Custom Farms contract. It is the standard boilerplate we've seen, but this is a big one. I already added some price and delivery protections, added a default provision whereby if they do not pay Milo on time he can require cash on delivery, and the limited exclusive goes away. But have Jim or Mark take a quick look and see if they think we need to revise anything else."

Jim and Mark were partners-friends of mine in our Omaha office. Or maybe more like friends-partners. Mark is one of God's works in progress and tends to waver off the path. He's a great commercial litigator but he's been known to bend, if not break, the rules on behalf of our clients. He has been accused more than once by our adversaries and opposing counsel of libel, slander, and various other forms of malfeasance. I don't like it when he does it sometimes, but our clients absolutely love it.

Jim is not much better. He helps me with my corporate and banking clients and he loves working with Kraig Nelson, a client of mine who owns adult book stores. But I swear Jim must patronize Kraig's XX book stores.

However, I found that together this attorney odd couple serves my clients very well in my absence. After many years of service, I have yet to receive a single complaint about them from a client.

"Have Mark focus on any anti-trust issues"

I knew Milo had little competition, and Custom Farms desperately needed his semen.

"And Eileen, tell Milo he must have Custom Farms pre-pay $750,000 up front as a deposit and can burn it off in year four and a half. As discussed, I'm concerned about Milo getting paid."

"Got it. No wonder our clients love you so much, Rob"

"And one other thing. Jim and Mark can, but you can't bill Milo for your time and advice."

"Rob, you know I know that, and so do our clients. That's why they love working with just me, too!"

"One more thing, Ms. Perry Mason, Esquire, can you do some research on Stanley B. Manilow here in our Atlanta office? I've met him a few times, like at our firm retreats. For some reason, he called me offering to help if I ever needed it. I guess I already have."

"Help? What?"

"Nothing."

"Rob, that's weird. He called here, too, late yesterday asking for you. He did not say what he wanted but asked me to have you call him. I sent you an email this morning."

"Sorry, I have not kept up-to-date on all my emails since yesterday, but that *is* weird."

"Yeah, so I already looked him up through my various sources. I can do more, but I found something very interesting, Rob."

"What?"

"Mr. Manilow attends Jak's church."

†

It was almost 2:00 p.m. so I headed up to the Coliseum on the top floor. What a spectacular view, especially from the lobby area. Even eighty stories above downtown Atlanta, the security windows were one-way. We could see out, but no one was going to see in. The skyline and architecture were even more stunning from up here. I looked down on the world's splendor and barely saw God's small children moving about for better or worse. From up here, all the tiny moving dots all looked the same. From God's view—we are.

As I approached a gray-haired woman I could tell that this receptionist was all business. Behind her was a large photo of the late Steven McGill, and she may have been our firm founder's first assistant.

"And you are?" she asked sternly and in a deep voice.

"Rob Ross."

"Robinson S. Ross? From our Omaha office?"

"Yes."

"Here to see?"

"Stan."

"Stanley B. Manilow?"

"Uh, yes."

"Just a second." She pointed to the visitor check-in registration, so I signed in.

Her nameplate was engraved in gold on her immaculate granite, desk. Ruth Ordare.

"Mr. Manilow says you can enter. Here, I'll unlock the door." She pushed a button releasing the door lock, and the tall vault-like door opened. "You are now allowed to enter, Mr. Ross."

My gosh! What was I getting into? What was Jak getting into?

Stan had files and papers out on the table as I entered the vault, er, Coliseum. The view outside was much more modest through smaller, tinted one-way windows.

"Hey, Rob, sorry about this morning, but I had no choice."

"Stan, what the hell is going on?" I could not refrain from yelling once the door closed. The strain of the day was getting the better of me.

"Jak is in big trouble. I told him not to call you, but he knows you are smart and help people."

"So, how is he in trouble?"

"He is saving souls, right?"

"Yes."

"Well, *these people* want to stop him. *These people* don't like Jak's plans to go viral via social media and televangelism. They have already fingered him to be one of the brightest young pastors in the country with the potential to save millions of souls and give them eternal salvation in the Kingdom."

"That should be a good thing, but who are *these people* I keep hearing reference to?" I asked.

"Their motive is totally opposite. Jak wants to explain to you."

"Wait a minute. How in the hell do you know Jak? Let me guess. You go to his church."

"Yes, I do, and I figured you would know by now. You're very smart and help people."

"So Jak is your pastor?"

"Yes," Stan affirmed, proudly.

"Does he know you killed a man today?" I was overwhelmed with the situation and couldn't help but challenge him.

"No, not yet."

Swell. "So why did you have to do it?"

"Because *these people* will stop at nothing to stop savers of souls, and Jak is doing just that. And he looks capable of doing it very well, very long. They have a lot of resources, and I wanted to send them a message that we *will* fight back. And please understand Rob, *these people* are definitely going to try to kill you."

I brushed that thought aside as soon as possible.

"So, who are *these people,* and why do they want to stop the saving of souls?"

"Jak will tell you more, but their objective is not eternal salvation for others but eternal damnation. They follow Satan, who has promised them if they prevent people from following Jesus and accepting him as their Savior, then they will live in eternity above the ring of fire. And rather than just going after individual believers, they have begun to focus on the leaders who are saving the believers. They figure without Christian leaders saving souls, they can more easily prey on the un-led people and please their own leader as the number of saved souls is decreased."

"So are *these people* atheists?"

"No. Jak says they are much worse. Most atheists are neutral and leave us alone. *These people* go on the offensive, and want to un-save us and stop people like Jak from trying to help us."

"So Jak's reward for doing a good job already is that he is a target of theirs?"

"You are a great lawyer and your son, no surprise even at his age, is a great pastor and can save a lot of souls. Rob, he is now their *main* target."

Damn.

"So they must have approached Jak."

"Yes," Stan offered.

"And?"

"They offer soul savers a chance to stop and join their forces and share the promise of living above the fire forever, or at least cease saving others."

I tried to think this through. "So they give Jak a chance to agree to stop saving souls, and they will spare his short life here on Earth?"

"Yes, but they do it in steps in order to gain credibility, so they first threatened to go after Shelly if he did not agree to stop." Shelly is another one of God's works in progress, and Jak's lovely new bride. She had also become Jak's pet project to protect along the path.

"My God, they just got married and started their lives for the Kingdom together." I thought about how I would have felt if someone had threatened Sheryl shortly after we were married. For that matter, how I'd feel if someone threatened her now. I knew Jak was strong in his faith, but this might have been asking too much.

"Yes, *these people* know that."

"So what did Jak do?"

"He called me and asked me to help. He somehow knew not to call you yet. I joined Jak's church three Sundays ago, and he and I connected in a matter of days."

"Really? It took me years."

"I advised Jak to ask for some time to make a decision. In his mind, there was no decision to be made. He told me he'd rather die himself than stop pursuing his calling of steering people toward Jesus. But I told him to buy us some time, Rob, I mean, we *are* talking forever here, right?"

"Go on," I said impatiently.

"Jak was able to get them to give him one week from yesterday."

"Okay," I mumbled, not believing my last twenty-four hours. Just last night I was relaxing with the dogs watching March Madness, and even the thunderstorm passed innocently.

"But they made his one-week window extension subject to one big condition."

"What?"

"He have absolutely no contact with you."

"What? Why?"

"They know you're smart and can help people."

"Did he agree?"

"He had to."

"Did he know the ramifications if he contacted me?"

"No, not at the time. But by now, they knew I was enlisted by my new pastor to help. I actually have an inside source with *these people* who told me to expect a call from one of *these peoples'* leaders. Sure enough, they called me and told me the deal they made with Jak. They explained that they needed to exclude you because you could help Jak. I knew that. But they then informed me that if Jak contacted you, they would first seek you out to kill you. As you know, Rob, they did."

"Yes, and thanks again. Now what?" I asked.

"They will stay after you, hoping to still convert Jak to join their forces as a super-star soul destroyer." Stan took a deep breath and looked me straight in the eye to make sure I heard him. "Rob, their plan is to kill you by the week's end, and then they'll go back to a crushed, weakened soul saver and again try to convince Jak to cross over, or at least stop his calling."

"I am ready to go whenever God calls, but would they then stop?" I was willing to give up my life for my son, but I wasn't certain that would be enough to satisfy *these people*.

"You know the answer. I understand your love for your son and your hope that you could end this, but of course not. If they kill you and Jak still does not stop saving souls even after yours is secured at Jesus's side, they will make sure Jak joins you in the Kingdom prematurely, knowing he'll never save another soul."

"I need to go to Jak's," I said.

"Yes, but you need to ditch the rental. It's not safe."

"Why…never mind. How do we *ditch it?*"

Stan matter-of-factly said that we just leave it. "I hope there's nothing in it you need."

"I brought all my work stuff up with me, but my clothes are in there."

Stan said without any emotion, "They're not your clothes anymore. Anything else?"

"Just some toiletries and my favorite electric razor, but let me guess, it's not mine anymore either."

"Nope."

"So how do I get to Jak's? He's down near McDonough."

"He's my pastor—I know where he lives and I called him this morning. I told him not to take any calls except mine until we get there."

"We?"

"Yes, I am taking you."

"Okay," I sighed in exasperation. I was in over my head. "Is your pickup safe?"

"Safer than your rental, but no, it's probably not mine anymore either. That's why I drove my old pickup. I'll see if we can borrow Dan's car. Do you know Dan? Dan Runner?"

I had met Dan at one of the firm's retreats. Law firms often go to retreats so partners can get to know each other better, including their respective expertise so they can cross-sell clients. The retreat where I met Dan was a doozy, as I recall, at the luxurious, exclusive Biltmore in Phoenix. I learned that Dan usually was crazy sober, but not that weekend. Crazy, yes, but not sober. Bad combo. Somehow, one night he ended up in one of the swimming pools with a giant queen the guests had been playing with at the courtyard's lawn chess game. No wonder Dan had never made partner. Checkmate.

"He's the single loner who lost his life-sized chess queen in the pool in Phoenix, right?"

"Yes, that's him."

"Helps you on some cases though, doesn't he?"

"Very much so. It can be an advantage having a crazy lawyer with little to lose on your side sometimes."

Stan dialed Dan.

"What's up, Stan?" Our firm's phones had not only Caller ID, but cameras and monitors so the attorneys could see each other. Dan's video monitor was off.

"Dan, close your door and take me off speaker," Stan commanded.

"Sure just a sec, but there's hardly anyone here now." Friday afternoons were when law firms tended to thin out. "Okay, door closed and off speaker."

Stan was still on speaker in the mighty Coliseum. "I'm with a new client of ours. Details later, but can I borrow your car for the weekend?"

I remembered Dan telling me in Phoenix, after about seven beers turned his brain on low and his tongue on high that he lived in a downtown loft, not far from the office. He often walked and just left his car in the garage. He went on to tell me more than I needed to know. My God, he told me he had killed some of Stan's clients' adversaries.

"Um," Dan was thinking, which was dangerous. "I don't think I'll need it, but if I need wheels can I borrow yours?"

"I wouldn't do that if I were you."

"Why not? Oh, never mind. Sure, you can use my Jag. Just stop by and get her keys."

We picked up our papers and briefcases and left the Coliseum. We stopped on the twenty-third floor to see Dan. The place was pretty empty and quiet. A few secretaries and stray attorneys remained, but most desks and offices were now empty until Monday. Dan and I shook hands, but the pleasantries were brief and much more serious than normal. Dan was six foot four inches about 160, maybe. Rough around the edges, but an effective lawyer/private investigator or hit man? I would keep him on task, if not on the path.

"Here you go, buddy," Dan said as he handed Stan the keys.

"Dan, if we need your help, think you could come down to McDonough this weekend?"

"Sure, I can always bring my pickup."

It seemed like every middle-aged man in Georgia had a backup pickup.

"Great Dan, also, I have my .45, but do you have an extra revolver or something Rob can borrow?"

Dan unlocked his credenza, and good grief, he had more weapons and ammo than your average pawnshop. "Which one do you want, Rob?" Dan asked me.

"I have no fricking idea, I don't even own one!"

"Give him the Colt Peacemaker. It's a single action revolver, Rob, and I can show you how to use it later. Give him a full box of ammo, Dan, and an ankle holster, too."

"Here you go. It's not loaded. Anything else?" Dan gave me the supplies.

"Where the hell do I put this stuff?" I asked too loudly.

"In your briefcase, Einstein," Stan retorted. "Remember, you're smart, and now you can really help people, but don't load it yet."

"Einstein doesn't know how to load it yet. Where's your .45 anyway?" I shot back.

"Same place yours will be when you're ready, but mine is loaded."

Swell.

"And by the way, mine is also a .45 Colt Peacemaker. So when I teach you how to use yours, you'll know how to use mine."

Great. "Dan, make sure you keep track of all your costs and expenses so the firm can reimburse you."

"What?" Dan asked.

"You'll understand. I also need you to open a new file for our new client." I had asked Stan to handle the formalities of Jak's new account with the firm. But Jak was actually already a client.

"Sure, what's the name?"

"Jak Ross. Just use my address for now, and tell accounting I'll be in touch with a special billing arrangement. For conflicts of interest purposes, the adverse parties are at this time unknown and perhaps unlimited."

"Got it. Hey Stan, you *will* take good care of her, right?" Dan pointed to the Jag's keys.

"Don't worry, Dan. We'll get reimbursed for everything. Let's get going, Rob. Dan, as usual, thanks for everything, so far."

Finally on our way to Jak's, Stan hit the twenty-second floor elevator button. "Why twenty-two?" I asked.

"We need some spare plates."

"Plates?" Once again I was confused.

"Yes, some license plates for her."

"Her?"

"Yes, *these people* are now watching our every step, and I can't let them trace us back to Dan, so we need different plates for the Jag."

"Makes sense, but let me guess, you just happen to have some extra plates lying around ready to install and throw the bad guys off?"

"Actually, we do. The firm employees know I collect outdated plates and in my spare time, I cut and bend them into nice custom-made dustpans. A lot of people keep their old plates and some put them in the garage or whatever, but at McGill Hecker, I tell them I not only make license plate dustpans, but I also recycle the ones I do not use."

I challenged his Christianity here. "So you lie to them?"

"No. I do make dustpans, and I either really do take them out with my beer cans, or I 'recycle' them on vehicles I do not want traced to me, or what I am driving."

"So, why floor twenty-two?"

"I've convinced a young associate that these old plates can be viewed as art. She fell for it easily, trying to do whatever to please a partner."

"I do get that."

We got off on twenty-two and entered the young associate's office. Again, a nice office for an associate just learning how to manufacture wisdom widgets and bill way too many hours a week. Ornate, dark wooden desk and credenza, state-of-the-art computer hardware, and phone. Like most offices, she had some real art and pictures hanging among the diplomas, but she also had outdated license plates adorning her office.

Stan said "I've been waiting to use this one." He picked up two Georgia plates from a shelf, with the personalized *Catch 22*.

"Why these, other than this office is on this floor?" I asked.

"I remember the bastard who had killed one of our secretaries, and he had these old plates. I got them when they were subpoenaed in his trial. He got off and out due to an incompetent prosecutor and a technicality, and renewed new plates with the same by-line. If *these people* trace these plates back to him, well so be it."

We went down to the garage. Stan explained that his pickup was on the third floor of the garage, the prestige floor, same as the third floor lobby and food court. Dan's Jag was on the first, so if *these people* were watching Stan's pickup they would not see us exit the garage. Stan surveyed the first floor and we saw nothing out of the ordinary. Pretty quiet actually. He quickly installed the *Catch 22* plates on Dan's Jag. She was beautiful. Pitch-black with tinted dark windows, plush Corinthian leather, and all the bells and whistles. She even smelled nice and new.

As we exited the garage Stan stopped at the gate and gave the attendant Dan's plates and asked to have them delivered to Dan Runner up on twenty-three at McGill Hecker. We could not leave the Jag's real plates in the car or anywhere *these people* could find them and trace them back to Dan. We were now driving a Jag whose plates would lead *these people* to a bastard who killed one of our secretaries. Maybe he would not get off after all.

It was bright daylight as we headed out to get on South I-75 to Jak's, but I squinted and said, "This car is so sweet, but it is hard to see out of the tinted windows."

"You get used to it. And it is sure nice to know it is virtually impossible to see in the windows." I understand the tinting to tame the sun but, until now, I never needed to not allow someone to see in.

We turned onto MLK Street, where I had parked my rental, to pick up I-75. Sirens and a fire truck were up ahead, but off to the side so we could proceed.

"Oh my, Jesus Ch…!" I gasped.

"What?" Stan yelled

There was little left of the leased Lexus literally incinerating on the concrete street curb. I knew the make and model but I'm sure most folks could not identify it now.

My heart stopped, I could barely speak.

"Calm down. That's where you parked your rental car?" I could only nod. Are you kidding me? Two attempts on my life, but saved for now.

We would learn that *these people* had jerry-rigged the rental to explode the next time someone tried to start it. The media later reported that some lucky visitor from Nebraska had rented it, but some unlucky thief who tried to hotwire it, was dead. *These people* got their wires crossed. The left hand didn't know what the right was doing. After one of them wired the car to blow up, another unknowingly tried to steal it. Two wrongs turned out all right.

Neither one of us said a word for several minutes.

Stan broke the ice. "Do we need to stop and get you some clothes?"

"No. Let's get to Jak's, dammit!"

4

I know there are a lot of good things about computers and the Internet. But I also fear that information overload (including much that is simply not true or accurate) might someday destroy us. Some people think it is already happening. And to think that the bad guys use it just as much (and just as well) as the good is downright scary. I'm afraid we are moving toward information transparency.

There are many entities and people who have the technology and tools to tell what you are thinking and intending to do by tracking and monitoring almost every action. The people who have this technology include a lot of folks I am not sure I trust. Our federal government is one of the worst offenders in the many ways they tap into our data and devices for both honorable and suspicious reasons. Others with this ability include *these people*, collection agencies, corporate espionage companies or just clever corporate marketing agencies, private investigators working for divorce attorneys, and even companies who specialize in locating brand new identities and locations of people within the federal witness protection program.

My gosh, they can track us easily. These entities have the capability to not only monitor every call or text you send or receive on your cell phone, iPod, or iPhone, but, in some cases, they can also see or hear the content and substance of the data or conversation. You might as well assume that every computer, laptop, and electronic or mobile device you use is open to the public. Everything you send, receive, visit, or practically think is available to the public, or at least any amateur hacker. Almost anyone can tell what websites you wander to. And, since over 90 percent of what we spend our money on now is via credit or debit card, or even by smart phone, it is easy to tell what you spend most of your money on.

They can input all of this data into super computers and see how your actions have been trending and, with scary accuracy, they can predict how you will act in the future. They are very close to taking the next step to predict what you are thinking, or wanting.

When you walk into Walmart or Wendy's, they already know what you want. Wow. Only God needs to know all of this. If people can ever know what other people are thinking? Seriously? Let that thought sink in for a moment. On second thought, don't.

I suppose ever since man stood upright he has kept advancing. The Luddites were British textile artisans who in the early 1800s, using sledge hammers and the like, smashed the recently invented mechanized looms. Their livelihoods threatened by machines and low-wage, unskilled labor, the artisans began protesting and spreading their machine-busting across central England. But their futile protests and attempts to slow technology soon ended and the Industrial Revolution rolled on, much like the Technological Revolution does today. I do not feel that my livelihood is threatened by technological advancement given my age and what I do. Unlike, say for example, truck and cab drivers. Their jobs may be saved for now, but not for long—not with automated driver automobiles looming around the corner. The people who produced pay phones lost those jobs long ago. Robots are replacing real people. And, when one person can now do what it took ten to accomplish, what are the other nine to do? I am close enough to the finish line that I won't get lapped, but as technology advances and brings increased productivity with it, less workers are able to produce more goods and services. Businesses require less employees even as they grow. What will all the extra unneeded people do? I sure can relate to the Luddites as today's technology passes me by.

The Luddites. I wonder if they were saved.

I was going to make some calls. Sheryl? Eileen? Clients? But Stan asked me to wait until we stopped for some secure phones.

Jak's was about thirty minutes away, and I just wanted to regroup a little anyway.

It was hot outside, and I hoped Jak had air conditioning. Boy, did I have my priorities in order. I needed a shirt change, and I figured I could wear some of Jak's clothes. We are about the same size and shape–six foot, and about two hundred pounds. In fact, I had adopted some of Jak's hand-me-ups before. When he put stuff in the Goodwill pile in our basement, I would see what I could still wear as he tried to give away what I considered perfectly fine shirts, shorts, and shoes. Although we now wore about the same size in clothes, we filled them a little differently. Jak had discovered weight lifting years ago and had become very toned, hard, and chiseled. He is very strong. Inside and out, I guess. I'm a little softer, inside and out. At least I had a plan for finding some clothes, especially since mine had blown up.

I decided to google this thing, thinking a little knowledge might make it easier for when Stan tried to teach me how to shoot someone. I let that thought sink in.

†

The Internet has everything you need to know about almost anything or anyone. I've always hated that concept. I don't do social media. I don't follow Twitter, and I don't like Facebook. To me, a tweet is a noise birds make. To me, a post is something that supports a fence. A blog is, well I don't know what a blog is. I mean, who cares what some *friend* is having for breakfast, buying at the mall, or when they had their last bowel movement? Good grief people, get lives. Unplug yourselves from the electronic IV before you become a slave to your gadgets. The addiction can kill you, if a texting driver does not.

And make no mistake about it—Satan is all over the Internet. He influences people to participate in e-gossip, spread falsehoods, commit crimes, and much worse. It is no coincidence that the number one industry on the web is pornography, just ahead of identity theft and financial fraud. Satan often works his magic by making people believe they have a right to do something wrong. Before you hit "send" or "post" something, ask yourself if you could add this endorsement from life's referee at the end:

"Hello, I'm God, and I approve of this message."

Unfortunately, even more of Satan's idiots are initiated on the Internet.

Satan and his surrogates send some of those signals, hoping to catch you in a love tryst, or fuel a feud with family, friend, or foe. Or even hope to cause an accident.

How many times have you looked across the lane to see a driver fiddling with a phone? Don't let it be you. Don't be among Satan's sad statistics.

You could be driving along with your two kids and a neighbor's child trusted in your care. You adjust the radio, take a drink of your four-dollar-latte, comb your hair, apply some chapstick, and look out your windshield and windows and watch the world whiz by. Then you feel and hear it, that seemingly irresistible ping vibrates your senses, telling you your inbox just got hit. You look down at it, then over your shoulder and in the rearview mirror to check on your pacified passengers. A quick glance out the window to try and stay on course, and you can't help yourself and reach for your cell phone. Who and what could it be? I guess it can't wait as you click it on, take another peek at traffic, focus fully on your phone, adjust your glasses, and fight the glare as you type in your password. By now your heart rate and your speed have accelerated. The text was made to look like it was from him. As you look down to open it, the horn you heard raised your head toward the highway for a fraction of one horrific second. Too late. You have crossed the line.

The car seats, seatbelts, and airbags were no match for the Peterbilt Freightliner you had hit head-on. The four bodies were mangled and burned beyond an open-casket burial, but the iPhone survived just fine. Later, the police and the phone company detected that just before impact you had opened one final, telling, chilling text, for which you just could not wait. Ironically, its mundane message simply said: Nvr mnd

†

I learned that the Colt Peacemaker, or Colt .45, is a single action revolver with a revolving cylinder holding six metallic cartridges for bullets. It dates back to the mid-1800s and is still manufactured by Colt's Manufacturing Company. The US Military used the Colt .45, or similar models, since 1873 until the early 1900s. The revolver was popular with ranchers, cowboys, lawmen, and outlaws alike. It remains popular today, but most current models are bought by collectors. Yeah, some collection Stan and Dan have.

However, what I learned next kind of made me wonder why Stan chose the Colt Peacemaker. From what I gathered from various informative sources, the loading sequence is something like this:

1. Place the revolver on half-cock and open the loading gate to the side.

2. Load each chamber in sequence (original), setting the hammer in the safety notch when finished; or (safe and prudent method) load one chamber, skip the next, load the remaining four chambers, close the loading gate, draw the hammer to full cock and lower fully, making sure that the firing pin is over the empty chamber.

3. Firing the revolver is accomplished by drawing the hammer to full cock and pulling the trigger. The hammer must be manually cocked for each shot.

"Stan?" No answer. "Stan!" Much louder.

"Oh, yes?"

"You're not sleeping are ya?"

"No, I'm driving, but I didn't think you wanted to talk."

I waited for a few seconds, and scrolled down for more. "I don't, but why the Colt Peacemaker? From what I'm reading, it seems like it might not be the easiest to load and re-load, and you can only fire one shot at a time. Seems like a mismatch if the bad guys have an automatic."

"For amateurs, maybe," Stan boasted. "But I'll show you how to fire it rapidly by holding the trigger down and quickly cocking and re-cocking the hammer with your other hand. It's called 'fanning' the hammer. If I need to, I can fire all six cartridges in about two and a half seconds, and reload the chambers in about three," Stan proudly proclaimed.

"I can't wait to learn," I meekly replied and rolled my eyes.

"I kinda like it when you marinate your comments with sarcasm. Besides, if you prepare and plan things right, as I prefer to do, most *shootouts* or gunfights can be won with a single bullet."

Hmmm, like the one that killed my tail.

Stan pulled into a small strip mall. Why they call them strip malls is beyond me. You never see a gentlemen's club or anything.

"I don't need any clothes, Stan. I can use some of Jak's."
He parked in front of a Verizon dealer. "Let me guess. You
know the owner and this is where you pick up our super-
duper secure iPhones?"

"Exactly. I already have one, but we need some more for
you, Jak, and others. Stay tight."

Stan took only a few minutes and came back with a
small box containing three "stealth" iPhones. He took one
out and asked me for my phone. He had this gizmo and
wired my phone up to it, and then plugged another cord
into what I figured was going to be my new stealth.

"I'm uploading your cell number, email network
connections, Internet service, contacts, favorites, et cetera
onto your stealth. You'll have the same number and all
the apps, contacts and services you had before, but your
stealth will be absolutely secure. Regardless of the lack of
security on the other line, any call you make or receive, and
any email or text you send, accept, reply to, or whatever,
cannot be tapped, bugged, retrieved, traced, or the like.
This is cutting-edge stuff. We're even a step or two ahead of
the feds. You'll have all the same features like Caller ID, but
unless they also have one of these, whoever calls you or you
call, will not."

Kind of a punch back at technology advance actually.

"I kinda like that, Stan. Nice gizmo there."

Stan got back on I-75 South and had a call coming in.
"Hey there, what can you share with me?" The caller was
sharing something when Stan said, "Well, you know me, give
me the good news first." Several minutes passed. I figured
that it was good if the caller was sharing good news. But I
still do not like it when people talk or text when driving.

"That is all good, I guess. Now, the bad, please." Only
about five to ten seconds of sharing bad news passed, but
I could see concern and vague discernment in Stan's face,
posture, and voice. His driving even slowed down.

"That *is* interesting, but let's not assume the worst. When are they going?"

Only one second passed.

"Okay, Cherokee, thanks as always. Please call and share any new developments you can. Otherwise, I'll see you Sunday. Bye."

"Was that about Jak's case?" I quickly asked.

"Yes."

"Well, tell me the good news first, too."

"Rob, first I'll tell you a little about who just called. She also has one of these phones we provided her. Her name is Cherokee. You might have heard of her. She's a singer and performer, and I have represented her for years."

"*THE* Cherokee?" I wondered aloud.

"Yep."

"I knew the firm did some work for Cherokee but I did not know *you* did a lot of it."

Partners in law firms with offices in several cities can be like some remote relatives you see once in a blue moon and at every other family funeral. Though partners, you don't really know them, or what they do, on or off the clock.

"Yep. I used to help her on criminal matters, but I have also tried to get all her contracts, endorsements, and various legal and business affairs for years. A lot of her business-legal work is handled by the Alston & Bird firm, but I'm angling for that, too. She has a lot of business and personal legal needs right now, and I want to introduce you to her. She's a great artist, but I have to say we have helped her leverage that into multi-millions. She used to get herself in some trouble, and Cherokee and her late husband had needed my help with various misdemeanors, and even a couple of felonies. They sincerely believe that marijuana should be perfectly legal, and like many celebrities, they thought some laws did not apply to them. Anyway, I have been working with them on their estate plan for the last few years, and even more so with Cherokee after her husband died."

"So how does she fit in?"

"She moved to the Atlanta area a couple years ago. She lives on Augusta."

"*On* Augusta?" I wanted to clarify.

"Oh, yeah. Her house is on the course, and I watched the Masters there last year. Her backyard is unbelievable, and overlooks the eight green and the ninth tee box. Maybe you can visit sometime. Jak might join us at the Masters this year."

"Okay Stan, but how does Cherokee fit in? What's the good news first?" I impatiently implored.

"Cherokee shared with me a couple years ago that she was winding down her career. Only a couple concerts a year. Her sixty-year-old voice and body are still stunning and beautiful, but she has lost the drive that makes good talent great."

"I can relate, but get to the point."

"She somehow drifted into the throngs of a local branch of *these people*. She never intended to buy into their anti-Christian movement, but agreed to attend some meetings for a friend as a favor. They loved the idea of having Cherokee part of their group, with her fame and financial capabilities. At first, she found them almost interesting. She told me she was sure she would never be worthy to enter the good Kingdom, so why not at least explore the possibilities of the bad?"

I get it. A lot of people think you have to earn salvation through good works and deeds, and if you sin too much you'll never have a chance. But it's through God's grace that we are saved. We do not have to be perfect. Not even close. Thank God.

"I suppose she lived a pretty wild life on tour, huh?"

Stan nodded and continued. "About three weeks ago she made an appointment and came to my office. I thought it was work-related. But she explained that she learned that *these people* were planning on taking their movement to a new level she wanted no part of. They were going to focus on the leading soul savers and either convert them and convince them to stop saving souls, or *remove* them. One of their main targets was a new young pastor right here in nearby McDonough."

"Jak," I muttered with a curse.

"Yes, I learned later. I decided to attend Jak's church three Sundays ago, and now I hope I never miss another Sunday. His genuine compassion and love for others is something I've never seen or experienced before. His ministry is captivating. His message is irresistible. He is my pastor now."

"And also a client," I added.

"Yes. Anyway, Cherokee needed counsel on what to do. I told her I'd understand if she declined, but I asked her to do a couple things. First to start coming to Jak's church, but also stay infiltrated among *these people* to gather intel for us."

"Did she agree?"

"Yes, we'll see her on Sunday. She met Jak two Sundays ago, and they've had a couple lunches and meetings, and she, too, now feels compelled to help him, and I suspect, eventually follow him."

Perhaps a double agent, but on whose side?

"Stan, I'm following all this, but we've got to be getting close to Jak's, can you give me the good and bad news Cherokee shared?"

"Right, first the good. Cherokee attended one of their meetings this afternoon, and *these people* have decided to scale back their efforts to stop Jak for a few days. They have put the bounty on your life on hold. Their thinking is that if they let you visit with Jak for a few days, hoping you might be able to convince him to agree to stop saving souls. They figure you will try to reason with him and convince him that saving real human lives in the now is more important than saving souls in the forever."

"The thought has crossed my mind, but even if I were to go there Jak will never do that."

"I agree, but I like their thinking as it buys us a few days. However, *these people* are unpredictable, and they could switch gears in an instant, so we cannot let our guard down this weekend. One other piece of the good news—they intend to send someone to attend Jak's service this week and check out the both of you."

I quickly asked, "Does Cherokee know who they are sending?"

"No, they knew she attended the last two weeks and interrogated her about it rather intensely. She told them that she was keeping her options open and decided to coincidently attend Jak's church. *These people* wanted to keep her as part of their group as well, given her fame and finances. They asked if she would continue to attend Jak's services and report back, but they intentionally kept the identity of the other planned penetrators unknown to her. She learned that they were actually flying someone in from their Birmingham branch so that Cherokee does not recognize them on Sunday."

"So the good news is that my life may be spared for a few days, as long as they don't change course on us, and Jak's congregation gets a new attendee this Sunday. I can't wait for the bad news."

"Here it is. Cherokee learned that *these people* are also sending two of their finest on a trip to help further their cause against Jak. They booked flights out of Atlanta for Monday morning. She's not sure of their plans or intentions, but I do not like their destination."

"Where the hell they going?"

"Omaha."

"Oh… Jesus…."

Silence took over for a few minutes, as we got closer to Jak's. *These people* were literally wreaking havoc all over the place, and now real trouble might begin to brew back in Omaha. I planned to be back there Monday before they could cause any real damage.

"Stan, so this stealth phone you gave me is ready to go?"

"Sure."

After I called Sheryl and gave her the latest update, I dialed Eileen. It was a little after five our time but only around four back in the Midwest.

"This is Eileen."

"Hey, it's Rob. How's it going there?"

"Great. The meeting with Milo went well, and we got his contract signed up. He loved your idea about getting the large upfront deposit. Custom Farms needed semen supplied to six of their farms tomorrow, as I guess all of the stars are aligned for the cattle fertility gods to work their magic. No other distributor has the capacity to deliver, especially on a Saturday, except Milo. Custom Farms already wired the $750 thousand to his account."

I did not realize the stars were aligning, but let Eileen beam. Eileen was quite proud of her work, so instead of commenting aloud, I just quickly thought to myself how, had I known the full picture, I would have upped the ante for the overall contract price and recommended that Milo get even more money upfront. It's all about leverage.

"That's great, Eileen. Good work." She asked how things were going down in Atlanta. "Fine. The people are great, but I need your help with a couple of things."

"Shoot."

"First, try to get me a flight back to Omaha late Sunday afternoon or early evening. Just email me the time, flight, and confirmation numbers."

"Done."

"Second, see what you can dig up on Cherokee. You know, the singer?"

"Of course, but why her?"

"I'll fill you in later, but focus on what she has been up to for the last year or so, and see if she has shared anything of interest with the world through the various social media sources."

"Ok, is this for a client?"

"Yes. I think you know him—Jak Ross."

"Hmm."

"Yeah, again, I'll fill you in later. Looks like we're pulling into Jak's right now. Oh, but one more thing if you can. See what you can dig up on the Dark Angels, particularly if they have branches in Omaha and Atlanta."

"Okay. I've actually heard of them, but I won't even ask."

"Good. Talk to you later." *Click.*

Stan questioned, "What makes you think you will be ready to leave Atlanta by Sunday afternoon?"

"If things change I can always cancel, but I think I want to go back to Omaha and maybe tail *these people*, and see if they try to make any contact with my family. Can you see if Cherokee can join you, me, Jak, and Shelly for lunch Sunday after church before I go back to Omaha? I think we need to start mapping out a plan, a strategy, for our new client. We can work on it tonight and tomorrow."

I already had been.

5

We made it to McDonough, a charming suburb with lots of green grass and trees starting to bud leaves. It was mid-March, but it had already warmed up in the south. I was in long sleeves and jeans, suitable for the mid-fifties back in Nebraska, but in the eighty-five degree heat, I needed a shirt change. I needed to change a lot of things. Personally. Professionally. Spiritually. And where this madness was going

Unlike the rows of look-a-like, cookie-cutter type houses you see in many suburbvilles, these homes all seemed to have their own distinctive charm. They were older and most had clean front porches with multiple chairs or swinging benches. I thought that most must hold millions of memories, stories, and dreams. Stan pulled into what I assumed was Jak's place—right across from what I assumed was Jak's church. Shelly was on the porch on the phone, but quickly hung-up as we arrived and descended the porch. A gorgeous blond golden retriever first greeted us before we even opened the Jag's doors. It seemed a little anxious and not sure of us at first probably because it could not see through the windows. The dog would have preferred transparency, and me too. But it came to my door and could probably smell our dogs on me, so the tail was now wagging and its face seemed to smile and beg for more attention. I obliged.

Jak had always wanted his own dog, even when he lived at home. We always had dogs, and mine had seen me off this morning, but we did not let Jak get his own while living at home. Now, he had his Goldie.

"Easy Goldie," Shelly instructed the dog. "Great to see you guys," Shelly said, but her welcome was lukewarm, and her hug hollow. "Do you have any baggage or anything?"

Of course we do.

Stan reached in the back seat for his, "Just one."

Shelly looked at me and I just shook my head and muttered, "I don't have any. I'll explain later."

"Okay, well can I get you guys some water bottles or something?"

"Sure. Is Jak here?" I asked, looking around the yard and neighborhood.

She pointed and said, "He's over at the church. He wants us to come over so he can give you a little tour, Rob."

"Great!"

Stan put his bag on the porch behind the three-foot railing adorned with pretty, blooming potted plants. We headed across the street, and Jak saw or heard us coming. His office is directly across from their porch, just about fifty paces away. What a fantastic short commute.

Jak came out of his office and met us. He shook hands with Stan, and gave me a big, tight hug crunching a few vertebrae like a chiropractor.

"Great to see you guys, and thanks, Dad, for coming." His familiar grin was still there, and you'd never guess he was well aware that he was the target of the Dark Angels. But Cherokee had called him, too, so he also knew they had decided to dial it down a few days. "Come in, Dad, and I'll give you a tour."

"I'll hang out here and make some calls," Stan stated.

Jak's office was fairly modest, but had hundreds of books on the shelves and across his desk. His office was next to the front of the sanctuary, which was where the tour started. A large stained glass window behind the altar illuminated the room with ample assistance from the sun.

Both the artistry and the message within were beautiful. The image was a touching portrait of Jesus telling stories and parables to several admiring followers. A piano, an organ, and several guitars and microphones adorned the altar, as did a lectern. In one corner was the baptismal font. A light odor of incense tickled my sense of smell—so did several candles, especially after Jak extinguished them. The setting was perfect for connecting calmly with Christ.

"This is beautiful, Jak."

"Thanks, Dad. We've been blessed."

We took a seat and sat in silence for a few seconds. He prayed, and I strategized. Then we walked to the back between the rows of wooden pews and more stained glass, crosses, and religious art. Off of the foyer were classrooms and a crying room, for small children, or large funerals. We did not go up in the loft, which Jak said held another classroom with windows overlooking the sanctuary. We went downstairs to the worship hall where they held meetings and social events. A large, recently remodeled kitchen was in the back. Jak explained that part of his plan to save followers was to socialize and make them feel part of a fellowship. Potlucks with parishioners pushed and pulled people onto the path perfectly.

We took the back stairs that led back up to Jak's office, where Stan had just finished up a call.

"Well, what do you think, Mr. Proud Dad?"

"I think it's awesome, and I *am* very proud."

Stan asked Shelly and Jak for their cell phones. He explained why and how it worked as he took out his gizmo and wires.

All four of us took a seat and tried to relax. This peaceful setting had allowed me to take a moment to breathe in the midst of our crisis. I had wanted to ask Jak something for a while and took my opportunity.

"How do you know when you have saved someone, Jak? I mean *these people* must think you are saving sinners' souls."

"I really don't. It happens in a person's heart. The true relationship between a person and God is really only fully known by them."

"That must be frustrating for you to work so hard and love so much and not know for sure."

Jak grinned. "Not really. It is actually very appealing. See, a big part of it is faith." He looked at a painting of Jesus and fingered the cross he was wearing. "Make no mistake about it, I can tell when I *think* I have saved someone. A light goes on, the twinkle of an eye appears, coldness turns to warmth, their actions show new love and compassion for others. They miss hardly any Sunday services and openly share their faith with others. They become *less of me and more of others*. I see literal changes in their lives. Kinda like the song: *Lord, I want to be more Christian in my heart, in my heart, Lord I want to be more Christian, in my heart.*" Jak showed off his beautiful voice. I made him sound even better when I responded with another verse of the hymn:

"*Lord, I want to be more holy in my heart, in my heart. Lord, I want to be more holy in my heart.*"

"Exactly," Jak affirmed.

"Let me ask you this. Do you think you have saved Stan?" I glanced at Stan. He leaned up and looked away from his gizmo and toward me and Jak with his eyes squinting and his mind clearly unsure of itself.

He started to say something, but Jak saved him. "Let's just say I think Stan is doing well, and is a work in progress."

Stan shrugged as if to say *fair enough* and crouched back down to his gizmo. A genuine, if not intentional expression, since only God really knew if Jak was right.

"I actually have a lot of works in progress, Dad. A lot!"

"I can imagine."

Stan had finished and put his gizmo back in his bag. I guess he had retrieved it off the porch. He handed Jak and Shelly their new stealth phones. He held up their old ones and said, "These are now useless and completely empty of all messages and data whatsoever. But they can be recycled if you want," and he held them over the wastebasket.

"Oh no, don't throw them away," Shelly demanded as she took them from Stan. "Here, I'll take them to the recycler next time I go."

Stan looked at Jak, "Do you guys have a land line?"

"Yeah, at the house, but we don't use it much."

"Good. Don't," Stan said, leaving no room for debate.

"What about here at the church? It looks like you have one on your desk, and you probably have others, too, but that's okay. These are fine here. Just remember they are not secure."

"Not like our super-duper secure stealths," I added dryly.

"Let's head back to the house," Shelly suggested. "And I'll fix us something to eat."

As we walked back, Jak pointed at the house next to theirs, another charming house with a lovely front yard and a comforting porch. "That's the associate pastor's parsonage, where Shelly and I were supposed to live. But oddly, a couple months ago, both the pastor and associate pastor announced they were getting out of the ministry. It obviously shocked the congregation at the time. I knew them, and Chrystal, the associate pastor, tried to explain it to me. They left under weird circumstances, for which I think we now know the explanation. I guess they caved in to *these people*. Anyway, I interviewed here for the associate pastor's position and ended up getting the pastor's position and parsonage. The associate pastor's position has not been filled. You two can stay there."

I had wondered how Jak had gone straight from graduation to head pastor at the age of twenty-two, but I never asked or questioned, maybe because I did not want to temper his enthusiasm or pride, or maybe I did not fully understand or appreciate his talent and gifts. Maybe all of the above. Part of God's plan I guess, as Jak often says.

"You guys mind if I make a quick call?" I asked as we hit Jak's porch.

"No," Jak said, and followed Shelly inside the house.

"Okay, silence by others I'll take as consent. Hey Stan, you're sure these stealths are secure?"

"Yep."

"I don't know how long they may have been bugging my old one, but clearly they knew I was arriving here this morning."

"My guess is they were monitoring you for the last week or so," Stan guessed.

"Swell. But now they'll figure out they've lost that capability. I guess you've killed my tail and squashed my bug."

"Two small victories we'll take," Stan said.

Small?

I sat on the porch swing and went on my computer to check on a couple of commodities on the Chicago Board of Trade and then dialed Eileen. You'd think I would've wanted to tour the house but I was consumed by all this, trying to think two or three chess moves ahead, as I knew we needed a plan. In parallel, I needed to make a living.

"This is Eileen."

"Anything new with Milo?"

"Milo not only paid the firm's invoice for the last month by wire transfer this afternoon, but he gave us a twenty-five thousand dollar bonus! He is really appreciative of our work on the Custom Farms contract."

"Great. Call him back, and tell him to tell Custom Farms that the cattle semen industry is experiencing a very severe shortage of inventory. The bulls aren't in the mood to produce, I guess. The cows' stars might be aligned, but the bulls' are not. Milo knows better, but he's cornered the market with our help, and we need to maximize his leverage. He is to tell Custom Farms that the semen supply is very low and the market price for beef has dipped below the threshold that is in the contract we just did with Custom

Farms that allows us to either not deliver or renegotiate. The semen supply has dropped enough to eventually reverse the drop in the price of beef on the CBOT. This is an anomaly that the market will soon fix. The price of semen just got better for Milo. Tell him it's the perfect time to play that card. This is big enough that I can meet with Milo and Custom Farms to renegotiate, if needed. Eileen, if Milo does not deliver the semen to Custom Farms, the markets will catch wind, and the beef supply will eventually reverse course and dwindle. Meat prices will sky rocket. I hate going for the jugular when my client's opposition is in a weak position, but I have my ethical obligations to do so. I put that clause in the contract for a reason."

"But if beef prices go up, that helps Custom Farms, right?" Eileen asked.

"Yes, but only if they have the beef. No semen, no beef. I'm looking down the road a couple of cattle generations. We can help them be the only supplier in their regions. They are big enough that we can agree to extend their exclusivity to all of their territories. We won't meet with or deliver to any of his competitors, giving him the dominant position. Make sure they understand they will end up with most of the beef, at the right price. Custom Farms will eventually benefit more than Milo, believe me."

"And Eileen, tell Milo we have a lot of work to do, but I offer the firm's services for the months of March and April at half of the price, half of our regular rates. Tell him we appreciate the bonus, but if he agrees to accept the half rates, he also agrees to give me free access to one of his private jets if, and when, we need it."

"Wow, you never cease to amaze me," Eileen responded as she continued to take notes on my instructions, and then hung up.

We both knew that Milo had three or four planes on his balance sheet. Successful businessmen in the rural Midwest often own jets. Commercial airports are in larger cities, but agricultural conglomerates earn much of their fortune in sparsely populated rural areas, where planes are needed to transport executives (and canisters of cattle semen) much more efficiently than the security-conscious international and domestic airports. Commercial airlines simply do not serve rural America very well.

I thought striking a deal with a satisfied client to get access to a private jet might come in handy.

I also struggled with whether to warn Wanda, a partner in our Minneapolis office, to tell Wendy's to lock in some beef futures. Wanda is our lead counsel for Wendy's, the hamburger chain, and a big client. My advice, and Milo's actions, were about to raise beef prices, which would hurt Wendy's unless they locked in future pricing. I could wait to see where this would wind up, but ultimately I ended up warning Wanda and Wendy's. I convinced myself it was different from trading on insider information.

I checked my emails while still out on the porch. There was a nice breeze now and it was not so hot. I deleted some stale ones and responded to some others. A fresh one came in from Eileen already: *Milo absolutely loved your ideas with the Custom Farms contract. And he agreed to your deal. His pilots and jets are available, if needed.*

I hit reply and typed a quick message to Eileen: *Excellent execution, Eileen, again.*

Stan joined me on the porch and said he was going down to the convenience store. "Shelly also needed a couple of things. You need anything?"

"How about a twelve pack?" I suggested.

"Already on my list. You have a favorite? Anything else?"

"No, but thanks, Stan—for everything."

"Sure. I'll be right back." And he left.

6

I opened the screen door and went inside. The big screen TV was on, and I had forgotten all about March Madness. This is usually my favorite time of the year—when springtime comes and closes the book on the cold winter, when baseball season is just about starting, and every team still has a chance, when I can plant my garden, take the dogs outside more regularly, and enjoy the weather. And then there is March Madness. I didn't even proceed to the kitchen to join Jak and Shelly since I noticed that UConn and Iowa State were in overtime. The game went to commercial with three minutes left and the Connecticut Huskies leading by three.

When a man loves sports and raises three sons and a daughter who do as well, many pleasures and memories unfold right before his eyes on the fields, tracks, basketball and volleyball courts, and sometimes he can just enjoy watching them play out on TV together.

I remember one time when Jakob was about four-years-old playing in a mini-soccer game at the YMCA. I love to tell this story. It was mid-July and hotter than usual. The teams play five-on-five, but the little kids were falling like flies in the flaming heat. Eventually, Jakob was the only player on his team still playing, against three players on the other team. While he was battling them solo—three against one—he outscored them two to zero! Too bad he can't remember it like I do.

Another time he was a little older and playing freshmen football. I still remember it like yesterday, how in one game he intercepted a pass, recovered a fumble, and returned it for a touchdown—all on the same play! He was playing defensive end, and the quarterback rolled out his way and tried to dump a pass over him. Jakob tipped the ball and intercepted it. Then, while returning it toward the end zone, the ball inexplicably came loose. He fumbled it, but he had time to recover it, and still return it for a touchdown.

Sports can dial up almost any emotion imaginable, everything between the thrill of victory, and the agony of defeat, borrowing a cliché from way back on ABC's *Wide World of Sports*. I often think of how lucky and blessed I have been to be able to share sports and an active life with my family.

I went to the kitchen as Shelly finished making dinner. "Smells great!" Maybe I exaggerated. Shelly was only twenty-one and trying to adjust to life away from her parents and hometown. She was also struggling with being a pastor's wife and literally living a life filled with religion. She was trying very hard, and I gave her an encouraging smile. Jak asked me to follow him and gave me a tour of the house. He explained that it was owned by the church, but like many congregations, the pastor is allowed to live in it rent-free. Not a bad benefit.

Lots of nice, old wood trimmed the walls and covered the floors. Our house also has wooden floors. When you walked, that familiar creaky sound could be heard with every step. I recognized the old couch we gave them. Shelly kept a very clean, uncluttered house, and had it decorated nicely. I also recognized many of the photos on the walls, and I about melted when I saw Jak's baby pictures. We proceeded upstairs, and when we were in Jak and Shelly's room, I told Jak about the rental car getting blown-up along with my bag of clothes and things. I also told him about Stan killing my tail. His reaction was benign as he frowned and said, "Yes, I know. Stan texted me, told me it was ok to answer his call from his stealth phone, and then he called and told me." He shook his head, grin-less.

I didn't think either one of us really wanted to talk about it further at the time. "Jak, I don't have any clean clothes. Can I borrow something to wear?"

"Oh, sure. Here let me see what we have," he said as he opened their walk-in closet where everything was neatly in order—his stuff on the left, hers on the right. All perfectly folded or hung. Nothing lying on the floor or out of place. I half expected him to take out an index card and look up what he had to offer me.

"Just any t-shirt and jeans, or maybe some shorts will work."

"Well, why don't you just pick something out and put it on. You can wear whatever you want. There are clean towels in the bathroom closet if you want to shower."

"Thanks, I think I will take a quick one."

"All right, see you downstairs for dinner."

†

I showered and got dressed and checked my iPhone, still upstairs.

I had an email from Kevin Kavan, the in-house counsel for a large cut-throat cutting materials company. Karfist Corporation manufactured scissors, knives, axes, saws, cutting boards, and the like. My work for Karfist was relatively recent, and their files ended up on my desk when one of my prior partners passed away. They paid our firm plenty of profitable fees, but I hated working for them. They were the biggest player in their industry, had leverage and used it. Too much so.

Kevin's email boasted of more good news relating to an acquisition we were working on. I thought the news was actually appalling.

It involved the Duane Eppers acquisition. Duane was owner of a relatively small manufacturer of similar cutting utensils in Louisiana. He had the unfortunate fortune of falling into the cross-hairs of Kevin and the Karfist acquisition team.

Duane was retiring and wanted to sell his business. He had worked hard and treated his employees, customers, and even his vendors very well. Everyone liked him. For a businessman, he was too nice, but he still made a good living. Sure, he left money on the table, but he did things the right way. He was going to end up in the right place. I remember talking to him during our due diligence. I was talking to him directly because he did not have a lawyer. He had a law degree but did not practice, and he thought he could handle the deal himself. So, I was ethically able to deal with my client's adversary directly. We were discussing his employees' benefits and insurance, and how they compared to Karfist's. He explained that he could not afford to offer his employees full health insurance. But he did point out that his prior year's profit and loss statement had a definite one-time non-recurring expenditure for a kidney transplant for one of his employees.

I remember asking him, "So Duane, just to clarify, you paid for a kidney transplant for one of your employees from an organ donor?"

"No." he clarified. "I paid for the transplant of one of *my* own kidneys to my store manager in Slidell. I gave him one of mine."

I paused, and then immediately took Duane *off the record* and gave him some advice regarding our deal. I probably pushed my ethical obligations to Karfist. Moral beat ethical this time. Ethically, I was legally obligated to refrain from doing anything adverse to Karfist in its deal with Duane. Morally, I wanted to help Duane. To this day, I know I did the right thing.

My response to Kevin's email was something I had kind of thought might happen. Karfist was basically stealing Duane's business for a fraction of its value, and they were taking advantage of Duane at every opportunity. I called Kevin.

"Kevin Kavan."

"Kevin, it's Rob Ross."

"Hey Rob, get my email regarding Epper's Manufacturing?"

The email I just received included a series of emails where Kevin had basically beat up Duane on every negotiating point. Duane's company leased one of his small plants from his widowed mother. After his dad died, Duane agreed to lease terms whereby the rent was a little higher over market, but it was what was needed to supplement his mom's social security. Kevin wanted to renegotiate the lease to lower the rent back to market or lower before Karfist stepped into it and began paying Duane's mom.

"Kevin, a lot of what you want to do is kind of taking advantage of Duane, his mom, and his employees who have few options, and you want to cancel his local vendors and go with your national accounts. I get the need to save money, but isn't doing all of this a little heavy handed?"

"Rob, do you represent Duane or Karfist?"

I hesitated and a lot went through my mind. I was about to lose a lot of loot, for me and the firm. But, I had found dummy files my late partner had set up to facilitate some of Karfist's fiascos. Duane was not Karfist's first victim. I had finally had enough.

"Neither, Kevin. Karfist needs new counsel. McGill, Hecker and I withdraw from representation of Karfist Corporation immediately."

"What?"

"You heard me. I'll cooperate to transfer your files to your new counsel, but I'm done. Bye."

I've lost a few clients over the years, but I've fired far more. Using legitimate leverage is one thing, but when a client crosses a line that I will not, they become an ex-client. Part of me wished I could represent Duane. I knew I could help him.

†

Stan was checking out at the C-Store and was chit-chatting with the cashier, Mrs. See. She owned the place, and Stan had stopped in a few times and was kind of a regular already. He paid for his stuff and headed out to the Jag. When he exited the store, he saw two men hanging out by his car doing something. "What the hell you guys doing around my car?" Stan lightly yelled.

Both men turned around to face Stan and froze, like they were picked off first base and didn't even try to get in a pickle. The short, chubby guy mumbled, "Sumthin."

At the same time the tall guy, who'd apparently lost his arm as one of his t-shirt sleeves was empty, was looking right through Stan with eye sockets that appeared nearly empty as well, and muttered, "Nuttin."

"Just admiring your wheels, buddy," droned Chubby.

"Yeah... I don't know about you guys, but I am having trouble seeing inside her." Mr. One-Arm-and-No-Eyes said. Here was Stan, a work in progress, up against lost souls. Stan did his best.

Stan motioned to No-Eyes to go over by the passenger side, and told Chubby to go by the driver's side. "Why?" said No-Eyes, unable to see where Stan was going with this. "We ain't got to do nuttin' you say, mister," declared Chubby. Stan bent over and put his groceries on the curb and, while he was at it, he grabbed his Colt .45 and flashed it for them. "I think you do," Stan shot back.

He kept a little distance between him and the Jag and took out his remote starter. He was just close enough that she would start with No-Eyes and Chubby at her side while Stan kept a little distance, behind a concrete pillar.

"You guys don't mind if I go ahead and start her up, do you?"

"Why?" asked No-Eyes.

"Go ahead, I guess," said Chubby.

She started without incident and Stan was as relieved as Dan would have been. The other two men were lost in the whole situation. They both had on black t-shirts, just black, short-sleeved t-shirts with nothing on them—no symbols, brand names, funny lines, or anything. Just plain black t-shirts. They both wore brownish jeans and dark tennis shoes.

"You guys just get off your shift loading boxes on the dock at UPS, or what?"

"What?" asked No-Eyes.

Chubby asked, "Buddy, do you smoke? You know, like the good stuff? You want some?"

Stan did not answer.

"Do you guys have your own car, or do you just simply wander around in life?"

"Yep," confirmed No-Eyes, while at the same time Chubby replied, "Nope. So you want some dope or not?" Again, Stan did not reply. Was he contemplating?

Stan noticed that the only other vehicle in the lot at the time was Mrs. See's.

These guys were part of *these people.*

"Start walking," Stan instructed. "No, that way." Stan pointed down the street with very few buildings or anything else that could block his view of them for a block or so. "Keep wandering, if you must, but I don't ever want to see your sorry faces again. But wait, first keep them right where they are for now."

Stan cracked the C-Store door open and asked Mrs. See to come out. She came just to the door, and he asked her softly to take a good look at these guys, which she did. He then told them to get moving and leave.

Stan then asked Mrs. See if she had ever seen them before.

"No, never," Mrs. See responded.

"Thanks, Mrs. See. I'll see you soon."

He gathered his groceries and headed back to Jak's.

†

Stan came up to the porch carrying his groceries. I heard him, but did not look his way, as I was fixated on the TV.

"Wow, wow," I said as I took it all in.

"What, Rob?" Stan wondered.

"Iowa State, in triple overtime no less, just hit a three-pointer at the buzzer and knocked UConn out of the tournament and ended their season. As you can see, the Cyclones are going crazy and celebrating the victory, while the Huskies and their fans are absolutely crushed, and some are even crying."

"Don't you just love sports?" Stan asked. I didn't answer and I just turned towards Stan as he was carrying a bag of groceries and a twelve-pack of cold Colt 45 malt liquors.

"Nice touch with the Colt 45s, Stan."

"Hope you like them," he said with a smirk.

"Yeah, but they *are* kind of strong. I'll take one, please."

Dinner was about ready as we walked into the kitchen. Shelly put the Colt 45s in the fridge along with some milk and the other things Stan had picked up for her.

Jak asked Stan what he owed him. "Oh, nothing, Jak. This is on the firm."

I kinda scowled at Stan. He, like a lot of folks, tended to push the reimbursement envelope too far once in a while.

Stan shared his experience with Chubby and No-Eyes and reminded everyone that, notwithstanding the reported ceasefire for a couple of days, we all had to keep our guard up.

We sat down to eat and Jak said prayer. "Dear Lord, thank you for this food and company. Please forgive *these people* who are apparently trying to stop us, and please work through us to show them the way to You. Please help us help them find You through Your Son, Jesus Christ. May Your Son return again very soon. In His Name we pray, Amen."

We passed the food. Shelly was drinking a weird colored Kool-Aid, Jak a diet Dew, and Stan and I enjoyed our Colt 45s. Goldie was perched right by me kneeling on her hind legs with her snout about table-level. Those moist brown eyes surrounded by lush blond fur were a soft sight to see. I don't know how they do it, but most dogs, even ones who hardly know me, are attracted to me when I am eating. Somehow, they know I have a soft heart and a tendency to share my food with them. Sheryl disapproves because she doesn't believe table food is good for dogs and thinks it will make them fat and finicky, so I often kid with her that I am simply missing my mouth. Anyway, I slightly held up a piece of hotdog with some scrambled egg on it and asked, "Is Goldie allowed to have people food?"

Shelly smiled and Jak's grin grew from east to west as they knew all too well of my not-so-secret connection with dogs—my culinary connection with canines—and Jak said, "Sure, but just a little bit." I cupped it in my palm and lowered it toward Goldie, and she very gently lapped it into her mouth. I was rewarded with some tail-wagging and an affectionate soft head rub against my knee.

"So Jak and Shelly, other than the issues with *these people*, how have things been so far?"

"Well Dad, really good. The transition to a new pastor has been smooth, and everyone has welcomed us with open arms and warm hearts. And attendance at worship service, Sunday School, and Wednesday night Youth Group are all growing. Without an associate pastor, I am staying very busy, but everyone has been very supportive and helps out a lot. I've done a lot of baptisms already, and did my first wedding last Saturday. But, fortunately, no funerals so far."

"Are you going to hire an associate pastor?"

"The Transition Team is looking at candidates, and I have talked to a couple since they would report to me, but I have intentionally stalled the process. I just don't think the right thing to do is hire someone until I have a better handle on the situation with *these people*."

"Agreed. What about you, Shelly? I heard you found a job."

"Yeah, part-time at the pharmacy downtown. I do anything from deliver meds, stock shelves, to cashier, or sweep floors, but I like it. They are very flexible with my schedule. I'm also taking an art class online through Georgia Tech."

"Oh great. I've seen some of your drawings—very impressive."

"Thanks. Oh, and I applied to work part-time for this company that reads palms and foretells your fortune or future," She offered gratuitously.

When we were finished, Stan got up to get another Colt 45. He asked me if I wanted another one and I said sure. He reached into the fridge for the now eight-pack. Jak and Shelly began to clear the table when Shelly said, "I can get this. Why don't you guys go on out to the porch. It is really nice outside." I offered that maybe we should go get Stan and me settled in at the associate pastor's parsonage. "Does it have a fridge?"

"Yes," said Stan.

"How do you know?" I asked.

"I stayed there last Sunday night."

Jak asked Shelly if the key was on the rack, and she nodded. Jak got the key and we headed next door.

Stan first grabbed the eight-pack of cold ones and his bag, then he handed them to me, asking me to carry the Colt 45s.

"Um, I feel armed already."

"I'll teach you about the real thing tomorrow," Stan retorted.

"I can't wait."

As we approached the porch next door, Goldie was with us and trotted up the front steps. We all three then froze in our tracks as we saw the dog as carefree as ever nudge the door open and go right in.

Not only was the door unlocked, it was ajar, and clearly not for any good reason. Stan gave his bag to Jak, and pointed back at Jak's place clearly indicating that Jak was to take the bag and go back to be with Shelly. Jak turned quietly and tip-toed down the steps and headed back to his house. Stan handed his half-empty beer to me, and I slipped it back into an empty slot in the twelve-pack container. He gave me a palms down signal to stay put as he bent over and un-holstered the real thing. It was not quite dark yet, but getting there. "Let me take the lead," Stan insisted. *Click.* I saw and heard him cock the hammer.

He slowly led us further onto the porch as I followed.

With Goldie already in the house and the wooden porch creaking even as we tried to walk gently, I figured we were not exactly making a stealthy entrance. Stan looked inside the door with his Colt .45 ready and saw no one in the foyer. He turned on a light, and was far enough in to see that no one was in the living room either.

Pop. A shot came from the kitchen, and Stan was hit and dropped his gun. I quickly picked it up and not knowing what to do with it, I gave it back to him.

Woof, woof, Goldie barked out, and we heard rumbling footsteps towards the back of the house. Stan was okay and picked up the pace as we made our way to the back door, which we had heard swing open and then slam shut. Goldie was now growling and looking out the door window. We saw someone running away towards an awaiting car, and they drove away. Stan was sure it was Chubby. The red stain on Stan's sleeve was slowly spreading.

"You okay? He hit your left forearm."

"I'll be fine. It just grazed me."

Stan locked the back screen door, closed the main door, and slid over the dead bolt. "We need to secure the house, especially if we are going to stay here." We went from room to room, even through the unfinished basement. Stan's Colt hammer was still cocked, with me right behind him. The house was empty. Stan locked the front door, and we went back to Jak's, Goldie at our side.

Shelly and Jak had been watching out the window and joined us on the porch. Shelly looked terrified, but Jak not so much. Goldie curled into a blanket on the porch, now oblivious to what was going on.

"Stan, you're bleeding. I'll get some bandages."

"Thanks, Shelly."

"You guys sure we shouldn't call the police?" Jak asked.

"No, at least not yet. Even if they find and lock one up, there will always be another bad guy to step up. I think we need to give ourselves a chance to resolve this on our own. But we're gonna need a little help. I have a couple ideas I'll share with you once I've secured some help and worked out some details." I was understandably scared, but hoped to take charge of the situation for my son. Though he was a man now with a family of his own, it wasn't that long ago I was fighting all of his battles for him. Sometimes it is hard to let go of that parenting instinct, but I could tell that Jak was happy I was here for this battle.

Stan added, "Besides, a simple breaking and entering won't get their attention, other than some sophomoric Sherlock sniffing around, and we don't need that."

What about the battery and attempted murder of Stan? But I let it go.

"Okay, Dad, but I thought they were taking the weekend off," Jak said.

Stan again offered "My guess is they still might do surveillance, or maybe some of *these people* did not get the memo."

"How comforting," I shared sarcastically.

"Now what?" Shelly asked coming down the stairs with some bandages for Stan.

"How about we calm down and sit outside here on the porch. I want to run some things by you guys. Stan, make sure you have your gun ready," I more than suggested. We were probably all out of our element but someone needed to take the lead.

The sun had set, and as usually happens in early spring, the temperature had dropped to something much more comfortable.

"Good idea," Stan agreed as he reached into the Colt 45 container for his half-full cool one. I finished mine, grabbed another, and asked Shelly if she could put the now seven-pack in the fridge.

Shelly quickly returned and lit some candles on the porch. It could have been quite a nice setting if not for Stan's bandaged arm and the fact that *these people* were trying to kill us.

"Jak, I presume you wanted Mom to stay home to protect her, huh? Good idea, Son."

"Yeah, but I also know you are more effective alone."

He was right, in so many ways. In fact, sometimes I can be a loner, and at times I think two's a crowd. Again, I confirmed, "Good idea."

I had a call coming in; Eileen. "Sorry guys, I need to take this."

Eileen explained there were no seats available back to Omaha on Sunday. "None?" All flights were booked. I had an idea of course, but let Eileen go on.

"Rob, I called Milo, and you have one of his private jets at your disposal Sunday at 4:00 p.m. your time, at the private terminal. I did not know if you were returning alone, so I asked him to have the pilot plan on one to three passengers. I cancelled your Tuesday commercial flight back from Atlanta."

"You're the best, Eileen." *Click.*

I told Jak, Stan, and Shelly that part of my plan was to return to Omaha Sunday. And, it was now by private jet, better than any first class commercial. I would then return Monday or Tuesday to Atlanta to work on our plan.

"Can Shelly go with you? I think she'd be safer, and more at ease, and she can see her family in Omaha." Jak's suggestion clearly caught Shelly off-guard as her face was fully flushed. She opened her mouth to say something, but I cut in.

"Yes, she can, and good idea, Jak. There is no reason to put Shelly in any danger, and it might be good to take the possibility of her as a bargaining chip off of the table." I wasn't only worried about Jak's safety here, I had a whole family to consider. "Stan and you can continue with our plan here. But Jak, what about you? Why do you seem to have no fear of *these people*, and how can you be so insouciant and composed?"

"Oh, I have my fears, but mostly for Shelly and everybody else. I fear for the safety of others and for the souls of all. But think about it, Dad. When you have truly accepted Jesus Christ as your Savior and invited him into your heart as you go through your short journey here on Earth, and you truly have faith that either when you die or upon Christ's return, that you begin anew in God's Kingdom forever, what really is there to fear? If something happens to me, not a single tear should be shed for me because within a blink of an eye I will be in the Kingdom. That is why you always hear us ask God to send his Son again as soon as possible. And if I die before He returns, within a blink of that eye I will fast-forward to the Kingdom with all of those who similarly believed. We will be joined by all those still here on Earth whose souls are still saved as of that glorious day. Do you understand, Dad?"

"I do, Jak. I do. But you're human, and this has to get to you, too."

But for the circumstances, the night out on the porch could have been quite blissful. Birds were chirping and flirting, and it seemed like every tree had at least one squirrel not even trying not to be seen or heard. A slight breeze faintly fluttered the flowers. I smiled realizing that you didn't have to be in a church to find communion with God.

Stan returned from inside with a fresh, cold Colt 45. I asked him if he had two Colt 45s, and he said yes, but only one was cold. I rolled my eyes and went in and got my own fresh cold one. Everyone seemed to be getting tired as they stared out into the clear spring night, with the dim stars trying to share the night with the bright, almost full, moon.

I thought I would run part of my plan by them. I asked Stan if Cherokee was able to join us for lunch on Sunday.

"Oh, yes, she was quite delighted that you asked."

"After lunch I think we should have Cherokee go back to *these people* and tell them that Jak wants to meet with them. What do you guys think?"

"I don't know," quipped Stan.

"No," demanded Shelly reaching her hand out to Jak.

"Yes, go on, Dad," said Jak slamming the door on any debate and giving his wife's hand a squeeze.

But first Shelly quickly asked, "Who does he meet with and where? When?"

Stan offered, "We let them decide."

"I disagree. I think we need to try to manage the process as much as possible. We need Jak to meet with a decision maker, someone with authority. Jak, who contacted you?"

"He said his name was Natas. My Caller ID said something like *untraceable,* but he sure sounded like an authority figure."

"Okay then, we will have Cherokee tell them you want to meet with your caller, the great Natas. She'll tell them that Jak wants to meet alone, Wednesday afternoon at two on the west side of the water fountain in Turner Park. My hope is that, as a result, they will extend the ceasefire a couple more days. Stan, can you arrange to have Jak miked—something safe and undetectable?"

"Of course," Stan confirmed. "But will we stake out somewhere where we can also watch?"

"I think we need to, in order to keep the playing field level," I reasoned. Stan was already starting to warm up to the plan and added that he would go to Turner Park tomorrow and scope out the surrounding area and buildings to find a good location. He'd drive back to the office to pick up the gear for Jak's wire.

"I'll call Dan and see if he can meet me at the office tomorrow afternoon. Most of our toys are locked up in his office."

"Great, Stan, and can you see if Dan is available to come down here on Wednesday and join us, assuming Natas agrees with our proposal? And tell him to stop shaving." I had been working on our plan.

"What?"

"I want Dan to be at the park nearby as a homeless person."

"I see. Good idea, but not much disguise needed," Stan added, and then asked, "When should we have Cherokee make the proposal?"

I finished a quick, cold swig and suggested, "My guess is that *these people* will be expecting a report back from Cherokee right after our lunch on Sunday. She does it then. I am hoping we have everything lined up before Shelly and I land back in Omaha Sunday night."

Jak and Shelly had deferred to Stan and me for the last few minutes, but I could tell Jak was fully onboard, almost eager to take this on.

"I don't like this. What is the meeting for, to try to save our lives?" Shelly surmised.

"Hopefully, that's part of it," I explained and then hesitated.

Jak finished, "But I also hope to plant a few seeds that allow for at least some of *these peoples'* souls to be saved."

"Right. And we can work on the plan and prep for the meeting between now and then. I have some more ideas to run by you guys later. But I want to massage them and give 'em some more thought first. I also need to make some more calls."

And then it dawned on me. Damn.

We had a problem. Obviously. Actually, it's what we didn't have that was the problem.

Leverage. I should have diagnosed our shortcoming and disadvantage much sooner. My bad, again.

We had lousy or little leverage. What did we have to offer *these people*—something they wanted or needed, that we had and were willing to give them? Or what did they have and want to keep, which we had the ability to take? What did we have the ability and willingness to do to cause them to give us what we want, or do what we want them to do? For me, at least, it was to simply leave us alone and let Jak minster all he wanted. If *these people* were just neutral atheists we'd be okay. But they go on the offensive. Our big disadvantage was *these people's* willingness to do things we were not. The temptation to take off the gloves was growing.

Our plan needed help.

We would need help.

We needed leverage.

What they really wanted, we were not willing to give. Jak was not going to stop saving souls.

7

The porch screen door allowed us to faintly hear the TV, and I could make out that March Madness was still entertaining much of America. I asked if anyone would mind if I opened the living room curtains so I could also see the TV and maybe follow some games. Escape the real madness a little bit. It was getting late, but another great thing about the NCAA basketball tournament is that in the early rounds there are a lot of games, and the ones being played on the west coast go late into the evening, sometimes past midnight. J-Rod, our youngest son, had been keeping me up-to-date on scores via email and text, and a couple of times asked me when I was going home. He was returning to Omaha from Philly on Tuesday. He had several Division 1 basketball scholarship offers, but had decided to go to St. Joe's in Philly, despite my not-so-subtle wish that he would stay home and play ball for our beloved Creighton Bluejays. I am not sure why he chose St. Joe's, but he likes to kid around and he told me it is because he likes their mascot, the Hawk. The Hawk flaps its wings all the time, and I mean all the time—pre-game, warm ups, during the action, timeouts, halftimes, post-game, you name it. I remember when St. Joe's was playing in Omaha against Creighton a couple of years ago and there he was, the Hawk, flapping away with both wings. The National Anthem was coming up, and I heard a yell from the Creighton student section, *Hey Hawk, put your wing over your heart for the National Anthem.*

For the "Star Spangled Banner", that Hawk put his right wing over its heart, but that left wing kept on flapping. Resourceful, but I sure hope J-Rod didn't pick St. Joe's because of their mascot. He does some questionable things sometimes and I often joke with people that he is our smart one.

Shelly got up and said she would open the curtains and turn the TV up a little bit. Jak said he was going inside to get something to drink and I asked him to grab me a Colt 45.

"Make that two cold ones if you would, Jak," Stan added as if placing an order with a waiter.

"Sure," said Jak and he went inside.

"Stan, did Jak tell you that he is adopted?"

"No way."

"Way," I said as Stan tilted his head and gave that *hmm* expression. Maybe he was thinking that explained a few things.

"Yeah, we adopted him as an infant. Took him home from the hospital two days after his eighteen-year-old biological mother gave birth. Thankfully, she realized she was not fit to be a mother, but her choice was adoption. Thank God. She initially approached me as a lawyer to help her place him up for an adoption, but I told her we would be interested and referred her to another attorney. After a couple of years of marriage, Sheryl and I had decided it was time to start a family. We discovered it was not that simple or easy. We kept trying naturally, but pursued the adoption process in parallel. After a few years, God answered our prayers by arranging our adoption of Jak. I often tell people we adopted two kids, but I'm not sure which ones. Anyway, we never imagined Jak would come into our lives and lead us as close to God as he has. And I don't think he is done doing so. The adoption itself told us God answers prayer. But Jak has, in many ways, been leading us to God and Jesus ever since. He often does it subtly, and lets us find our own way."

"Wow, some story, Rob."

"Yeah, and shortly thereafter we had Jakob, and then J-Rod soon followed. Three boys were not enough, and Sheryl really wanted a girl."

Jak returned to the porch with a diet Dew and two Colt 45s for Stan and me.

"So, we also adopted our youngest child, our daughter, J'Nay, from Korea. She is a teenager now, and becoming a very pretty, young lady. She's also very intelligent, except when she insists on always running up and down our stairs. But adopting J'Nay was very different than Jak's adoption. We specifically wanted a girl, and we learned that adopting a girl internationally was a lot easier than a boy, because in many countries females are not as valued as males, so there are more girls up for adoption. We probably could have been choosy and tried to find a specific, perfect, little girl, but the first infant female introduced to us by the adoption agency was J'Nay. All we had to go on was pictures of a six-month-old Korean girl in decent health who needed a home and parents. We looked no further and followed God's plan. J'Nay was our only choice. It has turned out perfectly."

"I didn't know girls were devalued in some countries like that."

"Neither did we until we went through the process, but again, we are so thankful that God helped us carry out His plan.

Jak looked at me, and I could tell by his familiar grin that he knew I had again proudly explained to Stan about his adoption, and then J'Nay's. He also knew that I was very proud of him and that his adoption was part of God's plan.

I twisted open the cold Colt 45, took a swig and rubbed some of its cool sweat against my neck. I could hear that familiar music CBS plays during the basketball tournament, and then Jim Nance welcomed the audience back to the Madness taking place at the Staples Center in Los Angeles.

I could see through the front window that UCLA was up on Gonzaga by eleven early in the second half.

"What about you, Stan? Any family to speak of?" I inquired.

"No, not to speak of. Oh, I was married once, way back when in what seems to be a long time ago. It only lasted a couple of years before my wife had enough. She always said I was married to the firm. As you know, our profession can be very stressful and taxing on a marriage and a family. We never even tried to have kids, which is good, I guess." He was right. Attorneys often lead the nation in divorces and suicides. Not a good stat.

"I am sorry."

"That's all right. She deserved better anyway."

"No, I meant I am sorry about the fact that you have never enjoyed the pleasures of fatherhood."

Jak's grin was back.

"Being a parent can be challenging, but the rewards are limitless. Parenthood also helps you understand God's love for *His* children, but I guess neither you nor Jak can really appreciate that yet," I said.

I took another glance at the TV and could see Gonzaga was fighting their way back into the game and now only trailed UCLA by a trey. My team, Creighton, made the tournament again this year, but again lost in the second round. Nebraska did not even make it to the big dance. They had had a decent year by their standards, and were "on the bubble". Kind of like Stan.

"Jak, tell me more about the former pastor and associate pastor."

"They were actually a father/daughter pastoral team. You see quite a bit of that, more than I'd thought. Their names were Pastor Millard Scott and his daughter, Associate Pastor Chrystal Scott. Pastor Scott was getting ready to retire, and the plan was that Chrystal would become the head pastor. My first interview with the church was for the associate pastor position, and I would work under Chrystal. She also taught at the Bible College, and I have known her for several years. They were both always so passionate about their ministry and sharing it with others. I just could not believe or understand at the time why they gave it up."

"And now you do?" Stan asked.

"No, not really. I mean, it is pretty clear that *these people* got to them, but I still don't understand it. Pastor Scott? Maybe. He was retiring anyway so his decision to quit was probably a little easier. But Chrystal's decision to quit was less than clear to me. Even now, I don't understand it. She helped teach me and strengthen my passion for the calling. I looked up to her and admired her work, and I really wanted to work with her. When I heard they were leaving, I drove down here to visit them before they left for Michigan. When I arrived, the moving vans had already been packed, and I almost missed them before they left. I caught Chrystal right here on this porch and gave her one last hug and tried not to cry as we said our good-byes. She was bawling but I had to ask her why she was leaving. Of course, it was before I knew anything about *these people*, and Chrystal was barely able to plead with me to never let *these people* convince me to quit.

"She wiped her eyes and looked into mine, and pleaded, 'Jak, be careful, but I hope you never let *these people* do anything like this to you. They threatened my family Jak, and gave me plenty of evidence that they are ruthless and will stop at nothing.' She continued as best she could, still sobbing.

"'Jak, I'm sorry. I agreed to a deal. I could continue to make sure my family and I remain saved and they would agree not to try to un-save us or harm us. But in exchange I had to agree to two things. First, to stop trying to save any other souls. Secondly, Jak, I cannot help you save anymore. As a result, I had to quit the ministry.'

"So I asked her how she could really agree to this, and she responded coldly, 'I had to. If not they were going to kill Elijah! What the hell *could* I do?'"

Jak was now emotional, too, as he recalled for us how it happened. He said he embraced her, and her words to follow steeled him.

"Then she further explained that part of the reason she was able to cave-in was that she figured she and I would be trying to save many of the same souls, as pastor and associate pastor. She reasoned that since I was pretty good, there are probably not that many souls that she won't save that I won't either. She finally concluded and said she wished she could explain more, but couldn't. But with help from above, I knew exactly what she was saying.

"Then Pastor Scott came out on the porch and asked Chrystal if she had everything. She nodded and Pastor Scott locked the door, turned, and looked at me, and said, 'Sorry it ends like this, Jak. I do hope everything works out for you, son.' He then looked at Chrystal and ordered, 'We need to leave. Right now.' She gave me one last hug, and they both entered on the passenger side of the truck, and they left. I have not had any contact with either one of them since they left this porch six weeks ago."

Silence ruled the porch for a few minutes as we stared out into the darkness. Jak had told me about Chrystal and how she had mentored him at the local Bible College, and I knew she had a husband and three kids. Elijah is only eleven years old, and *these people* threatened to kill him if Chrystal did not quit. I don't know about Jak, but I could fully understand her decision. When you have been married a long time and have invested your life in raising a family, you can be very vulnerable, and will do whatever it takes to protect them. And I mean *whatever* it takes. For example, drop everything and fly to Georgia, have a rental car blown-up, possess a gun for the first time, and fight *these people*.

There was a part of me that wished Jak would see things like Chrystal, focus on the here and now, and give up this madness and find some other job. But I knew that Jak's profession wasn't a job, it was a calling from God, and there might not be anything on Earth that would make him renege on his promise to the Lord.

Stan finished off another Colt 45 and got up to get himself another. Mine was still half full. Somehow, I let myself escape back to March Madness, but I could only faintly see and hear it. Gonzanga had fought all the way back to within a single point against UCLA. They beat the buzzer, but not UCLA. It missed. Season over. For many Zag players, career over. The cameras were scanning the players and fans, some joyous, but some crying as Jim Nance stated the obvious: *This is why we love this tournament.* I am not sure if CBS gets more out of showing the jubilant celebration of the winners or the deep devastation of the defeated losers. I wondered what it might be like this time a year from now.

J-Rod red shirted this year at St. Joe's. They missed the post-season this year and went fourteen and eighteen, but will have their three best players back for next year. J-Rod has grown to six foot, five inches, and averaged twenty-one points and eleven rebounds a game, leading his high school team to consecutive state Class A championships. Some people will kid with me and claim that they are sure that he was also adopted.

Stan returned with a cold one and asked if anyone would mind if he had a smoke. We all shrugged and declined his offer to join him. He lit up a filter-less Camel and took a deep drag.

No one said much for a few minutes, but Shelly's sniffles broke the silence. She was crying, and no doubt overwhelmed, and I sensed she was weakening spiritually. Her limp, sad body slowly rose as she announced, "I'm going to bed and I'll probably cry myself to sleep."

Jak grabbed her hand and said he was turning in for the night as well.

"Jak, do you mind if I just crash on your couch instead of over with Stan in the other parsonage?"

"Sure Dad, but when you come in, make sure you lock the door behind you."

I nodded and also told him that I was hoping to work in a workout. I was going to go for a jog in the morning and asked if he wanted to join me.

"How about we get up about 6:30 a.m.," Jak suggested. "We can go downstairs in the basement and lift weights for thirty to forty-five minutes, and then go on our jog?"

I looked over at Stan with the cold Colt 45 resting on his oversized gut while he was taking another drag and asked him, "Stan, want to join us in the morning?"

"What do you think?" he snorted.

I looked at Jak. "It will just be you and me in the morning, Son."

Jak managed a grin and told us he would see me in the morning, then he went in to try to comfort Shelly.

"So Stan, why are you doing all of this?"

"Don't you remember? Jak is a client now, and I intend to represent him zealously, as should you. I want you to make sure you write down all of your time on this case. In fact, make sure your assistant, Elaine, or whatever her name is, does the same."

"Her name is Eileen, and she is not a lawyer, as you know. I am not going to charge my son for any help I provide, and neither is Eileen. Eileen charging a client is unethical and just wrong. And charging my own son for helping him with all of this would be a sin."

"Come on, Rob, you can do whatever you want with your time on this case, but law firms bill out their secretaries all the time, you know that."

"Well, I don't."

"Well, that is your choice then."

"That's right, Stan. Life is full of choices. Often just one decision between good and evil, right and wrong, can put you somewhere on a very long sliding scale. I think it was Lyndon Baines Johnson who once said something to the effect that choosing or doing what's right isn't the only problem, but it is also knowing *what* is right. I'm not always right, but I know the right thing to do in this case."

"Whatever. Besides, remember I am a work in progress."

"Right, and moreover, how do you expect Jak to pay our legal fees?"

"I am working on that. As you know, I am on the firm's policy committee, and I was able to get them to approve this file to be billed on a contingent basis."

"What are the terms of the contingency?"

"Like I said, I'm still working on the particulars. And don't forget that Jak is also my pastor."

Stan took one last drag and found a marigold plant to flick his final ash into and put his cigarette butt in an empty Colt 45 bottle. Then he asked me, "You're pretty much all in this Christianity thing, aren't you?"

"Yes, I am. It's a wonderful feeling. What about you? Do you think you will join us?"

"I don't know, I mean I've helped a lot of criminals get off, and some of the things I've done probably should have resulted in me spending some serious time in the slammer myself. Doesn't that make it kind of difficult to be saved?"

"No, actually it doesn't, but I will leave that between you and Jak."

"Well, Jak actually tells me that it is between me and God."

"Yes, Jak is right, but he can help you. For that matter Stan, I'll do whatever I can to help you as well. But Jak will tell you that God is merciful and forgives even those who are undeserving. No man or woman is free of sin. Not one. Religion of man never saved a single soul. No one has ever been saved by adhering to a system of dos and don'ts, but faith in Jesus Christ is what saves a person. It is very simple.

All you have to do is genuinely accept Jesus in your heart as your Savior. Good deeds and regular prayer and worship are all good and right, but that is not what saves us. Simple acceptance of God's son, and trying to live a life as a child of God ourselves, that is what saves us forever."

"But Rob, forever *is* a long time."

"I know that, Stan. It's forever. It's timeless. Jak has told me a few times that if you believe in forever, then life is just a one-night stand."

"Kind of like the song, huh," Stan said, "Who sang that anyway?"

"The Righteous Brothers. The song title is actually 'Rock 'n' Roll Heaven.'"

"How appropriate," Stan said.

"Yeah, I bet there are a lot of great bands and rock stars in Satan's afterworld. He'd be tough to beat in a battle of the bands."

"Come to think of it, you're probably right," Stan said as he stood up and stretched, saying he was going to check-in for the night. He grabbed what was left of the Colt 45s and headed next door. I was tempted to sleep outside on the porch since it was so nice out, but I knew I would feel safer inside. I locked the door behind me and got ready for bed. Jak or Shelly left a blanket and pillow on the couch, and I tried to get some rest. I could hear deep breathing coming from down near my feet. I leaned over and could see Goldie curled up on a rug by the couch. I have always found it soothing to have a dog sleeping nearby. They can hear every little sound, and the smart ones learn how to filter out the harmless, benign noises, but alert you when they sense something out of the ordinary or threatening. I started wondering about everything that had transpired throughout the day, but I did my best to block it out. I realized I had been up since 3:00 a.m., and I was exhausted. After prayer, sleep came fairly quickly.

I went into a deep sleep, but it was so late that the next day came quickly. Slowly, I began my way out of rest as the hours passed. My eyes were closed tightly, but beyond my eyelids was a faint flickering of light. Dark sleep still held its grip, but it was loosening, and the flickering was there, gently penetrating through my thin, closed eyelids. Not unlike heat lightning off in the distance. Do you really see lightning, or its reflection? The flickering light was becoming weaker and not as rapid—akin to the slowly, diminishing, final, shallow breaths of a person in hospice nearing death. I turned my head toward the window, to the flickers, and slightly cracked open an eyelid. The street light was dying, and its bulb finally went dark and died. Did it shine for its normal life expectancy, or did *these people* extinguish it?

8

Saturday, March 22

Daylight was growing as light was slightly penetrating the living room through the windows where I had forgotten to close the curtains. Jak and I got up early and lifted weights, then went for our morning jog. Jak told me that staying fit physically helps you stay fit spiritually. Discipline, he explains. Maybe he is trying to tell me something.

After about a couple miles, we stopped jogging and started walking on a pretty path around a park. I got out some gum, offered a piece to Jak, took one myself, and tossed the wrapper to the ground.

"Dad!" He picked it up and put it in his pocket.

"Sorry." It feels weird when your child corrects you and gets you back on the path.

I knew better, but did not do better. Dang it. I do that too often. Jak started jogging again, and I did my best to keep up. Jogging has many benefits, one of which is that it can be difficult to carry on a conversation when you don't really want to.

When we returned, Stan and Shelly were waiting for us on the porch, drinking coffee. We joined them. Shelly got me a cup of coffee, and Jak a water.

A police car pulled into the driveway.

Stan spotted them first. "Did someone call the cops?"

"No."

"Well, looks like we have visitors. Don't we all feel safer already?" Stan recognized one of the men that got out of the squad car. He apparently knew the uniformed guy from his criminal law days. He motioned the men to join us on the porch and greeted them. They came to the foot of the steps.

"Hey, Detective Crow. It's been a while."

"Yeah, which was fine with me, Manilow," retorted Crow.

"Who's your plainclothes sidekick?" Stan asked.

Even though it was already almost eighty-five degrees out, the sidekick was wearing a worn trench coat that looked like a third generation hand-me-down. His hair was short, black, and very greasy.

Sidekick proclaimed, "The name is Sergeant Tuey."

"Your parents named you Sergeant?" Stan asked.

I was able to fight back a grin. Jak was not.

"Still the funny man, huh, Manilow?" Crow asked.

"I can't help myself. But what can we help you fine officers with this morning?"

"I'll ask the questions, Manilow." Crow tried to take charge.

"Well, Crow, I see you still haven't seen that surgeon I recommended to you more than once a few years ago."

"Surgeon, for what?"

"So he can surgically remove that chip off your shoulder."

It was obvious that Stan and Crow had crossed many paths before. No doubt Crow testified in the prosecution of some of Stan's clients and had been subject to his cross-examination. Stan seemed to be warming up to the good ole days.

"Anyway, Manilow, we are here doing an investigation and tracked you down for some questioning. Your secretary said we could find you at your pastor's house. First, when was the last time you saw or talked to that child molester you got off?"

"Which one?"

"Pathetic that you have to ask, but the one who abducted the twelve-year-old girl and held her in his mommy's basement for seven days of hell."

"Oh, yeah, Gil Egan," Stan recalled.

"Yeah, that pervert," Crow confirmed.

"Why do you ask?" Stan asked.

"I am asking the questions, Manilow!"

"Fine, Chip. Keep firing."

"When was the last time you talked to or saw Gil Egan?"

"I don't recall having any further contact with Gil after his acquittal when he left the courthouse a free man. The hefty retainer he had paid the firm more than covered his legal fees, and in fact he told me to keep the excess as a bonus. So since his acquittal, I have had no contact."

"Yeah, it still gets under my craw that you got that maggot off."

"Your guys botched that case big time Crow, and you know it. A second-year law student could have defeated those charges. Your evidentiary chain of custody was compromised or even outright broken not once, not twice, but at least three times, as I recall. Your prosecutor failed miserably in introducing critical evidence against Egan. Your star witness was a twice-convicted felon who also had a perjury charge on his rap sheet. You could not locate another key witness, one whom we had interviewed less than twenty-four hours before the trial started. You guys have no one to blame but yourselves."

"It was a complex, complicated case, and we had a low budget for the investigation and prosecution."

"Whatever, but half the time the bad guy walks not so much because he has a good defense counsel, but because the prosecutors, detectives, and sergeants screw up the case somehow."

"Well, Egan won't be messing with any young girls anymore," Crow assured.

"Why's that?"

"He's dead. Shot once in the head almost execution style in the front seat of his neon-green car yesterday. A single .45 caliber bullet right through the head. Of course, we are checking all sources and angles, and thought his superhero attorney might have information on what went down, or who might have wanted to see him dead."

Uh oh. Stan kept his cool, just looked at the officers and didn't say anything right away as he quickly realized that they were investigating his murder (or killing) of my tail the day before.

Stan finally offered, "That's too bad about Gil."

"Yeah, the guys back at the precinct are deeply saddened," Crow deadpanned. "But a murder is a murder, Manilow, and even when the victim is among the scummiest of the scumbags, we still need to investigate and track down the murderer."

"Liberty and justice for all, huh, Crow?" Stan was playing with them again.

"So do you have any leads on who might have had it out for Egan?" asked Crow.

"Knowing Gil, you probably have numerous suspects, but like I said, I don't have any clues, at least not that I can give you."

Crow let that disclaimer escape him.

"Do you have any idea why Egan would have been armed?"

"No."

"We found a loaded Beretta, semi-automatic, at his side and these two odd photographs." Crow handed Stan two slightly bloodstained photos. Stan looked them over and tilted them toward me so I could see. This time I had to fight back a scream. One was a picture of Jak's church. The other was a photo of me.

Stan gave Crow the photos back and calmly said, "No, but that is odd." Stan may have been talking more to me than Crow. Neither one of us offered to connect the dots to the two large clues that were staring right at Crow and Tuey. They started down the porch, and Crow asked Stan to give him a call if any clues came to mind. They got in their trooper and drove away, clueless.

"Damn, Stan, did you see those pictures? It was Jak's church, and me."

Stan was kind of chuckling, "Yes, of course I saw 'em. And did you make out in the lower right hand of the frame the church sign, you know, the one right there?" Stan pointed to the concrete and marble monument sign telling the world: *Welcome to Eternal Life Church of God.*

"Those moronic Colombo wannabes did not even connect the photo with the church. Besides, all they had to do was google the church name, and that would have led them here anyway," Stan reasoned.

"And they apparently did not recognize me, but they will figure it out, and they will be back."

"Yeah. Did you notice something else odd about the church photo?"

"What, Manilow, I mean, Stan?"

"From where it was apparently taken," explained Stan, as he took about three steps across the porch toward the church, put his hands up in front of his eyes as if to take a snapshot and said, "From right about here would be my guess."

"How comforting. But why didn't you connect the dots for them, with respect to the photos I mean?"

"Well, I thought about just confessing and telling them that I am their man, but decided to let them spin their wheels for a while. And why didn't you?"

"I figured I would stay out of it since you clearly had it under control. But what do we say when they come back and question why we did not point them to the church and me?"

"We smash their ego with a sledge hammer and tell them that we thought it was so damn obvious we didn't need to."

"Okay, but did you recognize Egan yesterday?"

"No, I did not get close enough. I just knew *these people* sent a tail to kill you with no questions asked. If I hesitated, you were in trouble. Besides, remember, I wanted to send *these people* a message."

"Okay, but isn't it a big coincidence that you represented my tail, you get him off, he joins *these people*, he tries to kill me, and you end up killing him?"

"I guess."

But Jak now added, "Maybe not. *These people* tend to have a lot of criminals among them. In fact, they recruit them, especially ones acquitted because they are not incarcerated. They like to have some members on their team willing to do some evil things, if you know what I mean."

"Makes sense," I said.

"In the meantime, Rob, you *did* see Gil Egan raise his gun and point it at me right before I shot him, right?"

"At least Crow was right about something, Stan—you can be kind of pathetic. I'm going in to get cleaned up."

As I headed in the house, Stan yelled, "Fine, then I'll give you your lesson."

"Dad, wait a second. Stan, can you ask for forgiveness for a justifiable killing, unfortunate collateral damage in the battle between good and evil?"

"I think so."

"Dad, let's keep an open mind if Stan becomes a suspect."

"Okay." I went in to clean up.

Stan looked at Jak, who he was sure was bewildered by what just happened with the officers. "Jak, do you understand what just went down here, or do I need to explain?"

"No, I understand perfectly. I'm going inside, too."

"Jak, you know that since you are a client of the firm that everything said in confidence between you and me and for that matter, between you and your dad, is potentially confidential and attorney-client protected, right?"

"Of course," Jak responded.

"And you know what that means?"

"Oh yeah, let me explain. Dad has talked about that many times. He even set up firm files for each of us kids as well as Mom, and even billed us small amounts that we paid so as to make us legitimate clients. Just because your lawyer is also your dad or husband does not invalidate your attorney-client privilege. Dad claims that almost every word between us can be painted as legal advice if the canvas is big enough. That way, if necessary, he can at least argue that certain conversations of ours are privileged against the world."

"Hmm," was all Stan could respond as Jak went inside.

9

Jak and I got cleaned up and grabbed a quick, but late, breakfast. Coffee, toast, and some curd of milk coagulated and pressed into a hard square mass, in other words, cheese. Stan came in and told me to grab my Colt .45.

"A little early for that isn't it?" I tried to humor him, but he was not in the mood. Nor really was I.

"Not funny. You know what I mean, and bring your ammo, and holster, too."

"Jak, do you want to come with us for my lesson?"

"No. I'm going over to the church to work on mine. There should be a good crowd tomorrow. It's Palm Sunday," Jak grinned.

"Oh yeah, and next week is Easter," I added.

Jak's grin evaporated, "Yes, tomorrow starts perhaps the darkest week of the year."

"Jak, we'll be all right, we have a plan," I tried to assure him, although I was not totally sure myself.

"I agree. But what I meant was the week after what we now call Palm Sunday. It was during that week that Jesus was betrayed, beaten, ridiculed, vilified, and eventually nailed to a cross, crucified, and died on Good Friday."

"I always wondered why we call it Good Friday." Stan added.

It was a great question, but I had heard the answer before. Jak explained it again.

"Good question, Stan. That was the day our Savior willingly died for us, to wash away our sins with his blood.

He then arose on Easter Sunday, and ever since calls us to accept him into our hearts so that we can have eternal life when he comes again. It's called *Good* Friday because the goodness of our Savior's sacrifice overwhelms the evil that was done to him."

"I see." Stan paused and smiled. There was a glint to his eye I hadn't seen before. Perhaps he was making progress toward understanding and receiving the message. "We'll see you this afternoon, Jak. Come on, Rob, let's go shoot something."

Stan and I got in the Jag and left. As we were leaving town, Stan looked out the window and exclaimed, "Damn, check out that hot babe." I turned toward the sidewalk and saw a beautiful brunette baring bits of her body, but I brushed aside Stan's boorish lust. He kept any further comments to himself. I was above and beyond Stan's behavior, right? Right?

Jak's house and the church are on the edge of town, so it didn't take us long to reach a more deserted country area. Stan explained that he helped a farm couple with their estate plan recently, and he would ask them if we could do some target practice out behind their barn. A pleasant spring day allowed us to roll down the Jag's soft top and enjoy the cerulean sky above.

As he turned in, I saw that there was about one hundred yards separating the homestead from the road. Along both sides of the rocky road rolling up to the house were rows and rows of cotton and corn framing the lane with a welcome. The combined scents of livestock, growing grasses, and crops produced a somewhat paradoxical but palliative perfume—it actually smelled good.

To the right, the lane turned onto a concrete pad right in front of a three-car garage flanking the side of the stately old farmhouse. To the left stood a large barn with its front doors open, clearly showing the farmhands were hard at work. They were working on a John Deere tractor and a large weed sprayer. Behind the barn several silos reached for the sky, and the farm's out buildings covered nearly ten acres of land before the cropland fully took over. While the land was hilly, I could also see herds of cattle and a pen or two of hogs. The chickens were free to roam everywhere, and parted from the drive as we approached. They stuck around, even uncaged, due to the food source.

I could tell this was a prosperous farm and could easily see why the owner would have sought a good estate planner to protect their assets during the transfer. As we pulled into the place, two plump farm dogs that had been lazing in the sun near the house ambled over to lazily check us out. Farm cats were playing in the sun motes in front of the storm cellar door and hardly noticed us.

Stan parked and went inside to get permission. As I looked around, I noticed that these people were customers of Milo Schneider. Over by the barn was one of Schneider Distribution's familiar canisters that had once contained cattle semen. Stan returned, and we drove back past the barn waving to the laborers. The driveway, like all of the roads on the farm, was rocky dirt, and I thought what it would be like when it rained. Stan did not want to alarm the livestock with the gunshots, so we drove away from them down the lane to the far edge of the farmstead in between forty acres of more cotton and about 160 acres of soybeans.

We got out with our Colt .45s. Stan was explaining that most models have a longer barrel, but both he and Dan prefer the shorter barrel Peacemaker.

"Kind of like a sawed off pistol, huh?"

"I guess you could say that, but it does fit in the holster better," Stan reasoned.

He proceeded to teach me how to load the gun, cock the hammer, and fire away. He even taught me how to 'fan the hammer' a few times. We had brought some empty pop cans and placed two of them on a fence about twenty yards away. He came back, cocked, fired twice, and hit both with precision. He reset the cans and said it was my turn. I went one for two.

"Not bad."

Stan reset some cans for me, and I continued hitting around fifty percent. We continued for several minutes until the cans became mangled.

"So, you think you know how to use it?" he asked.

"I guess, but I'm not sure I will. But yes, I know how, now."

"Good. See, you're smart and now you can *really* help people."

I rolled my eyes, unloaded my Peacemaker, put it in the holster, and started toward the car. Stan holstered his at his ankle. I just held mine.

"Aren't you going to put it on?"

"No, I'd probably shoot myself in the foot, and I feel odd enough."

We headed back to Jak's. Part of me just wanted to stay at that fond farm for a few hours. The expected lifestyle, the routine, and the peacefulness of the farm appealed more to me than holding my gun and preparing a meeting with this devil-worshipper Natas.

Stan drove us back to Jak's, dropped me off, and headed back to the office to meet Dan and to get Jak's mike and some other toys.

Goldie greeted me on the porch, her tail wagging feverishly. I wished I had a snack for her. So did she.

Shelly said Jak was over at the church. Shelly explained that Saturday nights and Sunday mornings were lonely for her because Jak always had a lot to prepare. She was proud of her husband, but he worked so hard on weekends that she barely had time to spend with him.

I headed over to the church and found Jak working on his message. He mentioned that he sent an email to the congregation asking them to make me and *all* our visitors tomorrow feel welcome.

I sat down with him in his office. How odd it felt to see him sitting on the working side of the desk instead of me. It made me proud, too. "I know you've only been doing this for a few weeks, but I wonder if you have tried to save anyone who does not want to be saved."

He thought for a while, "No, I don't think so. But remember, for some people it's a work in progress. But I will say, for the non-believers who really do not grasp what being saved means, saving them will be very tough. However, I would like to think I would not give up on trying to save anyone."

"I'm thinking about Natas. I think we need to propose a deal. If you can't convince him to be saved within a year or so, you will give up your calling and stop helping people save their souls. Would you be willing to make that challenge?"

Jak sighed and pushed back his chair. He was thinking about my question. "He'd be difficult to gather and convince that Jesus is the way. In fact, he'd be the ultimate challenge. But that's a heck of a price to pay if I can't save him. But for argument's sake, what if I do convert him and he accepts our Savior as his?"

"He calls off *these people,* and at the very least, they mind their own business."

"That should be a given if he truly becomes saved, but if that is what you think we should do, I'll think about it."

"You might start thinking about how you help someone be saved who does not want to be saved, and in fact wants others to also be or remain un-saved."

"I'm not sure it's possible, but ..." Jak stopped mid-sentence.

"What?"

"Like I said, I'll think about it. And, of course, pray for guidance."

"Another option is that you suggest that if you stop saving souls, he will stop trying to un-save souls. You both stop. Think about it, net net—you might actually be the winner. You save less, but he un-saves even less."

"Hmm," Jak was thinking again.

"But I doubt Natas would go for that. So here's another angle we can think about. How many people do you think will make it into the Kingdom?"

"Well, based on what I believe, what we believe, if you assume the Earth is God's only creation containing his children, and there are say seven billion children, I believe less than one billion will enter the Kingdom on that Glorious Day."

"That's all? I'm not good at math, but less than fourteen percent?"

"Yes. Some people find this number to be too low, while many others find it to be too high. But most never find God."

"How unfortunate."

"Yes, and it's sad because I think it could be so many more. But Jesus himself tells us that a large majority of God's children will *not* be saved when Jesus returns. In Matthew 7:13-14, he tells us:

'Enter by the narrow gate, for wide is the gate and broad is the way that leads to destruction, and there are many who go in it. Because narrow is the gate and difficult is the way which leads to life, and there are few who find it.'

"And in Luke 13:22-28, we read:

'And He went through the cities and villages, teaching and journeying toward Jerusalem. Then one said to Him, "Lord, are there few who are saved?" And He said to them, "Strive to enter through the narrow gate for many, I say to you, will seek to enter and will not be able. When once the Master of the house has risen up and shut the door, and you begin to stand outside and knock at the door, saying, 'Lord, Lord, open for us,' and He will answer and say to you, 'I do not know you, where you are from.' Then you will begin to say, 'We ate and drank in Your presence, and You taught in our streets.' But He will say, 'I tell you I do not know you, where you are from. Depart from Me, all you workers of iniquity.'

There will be weeping and gnashing of teeth when you see Abraham and Isaac and Jacob and all the prophets in the kingdom of God, and yourself thrust out.'"

"Okay then. Jak, what if we proposed a deal where you would limit the number of souls you would save. Of course, you, Shelly, our family and friends, and we could propose that you would then limit it to your congregation, and I could draft an amendment to your church bylaws and constitution that your membership can't exceed a specific amount. I've been thinking this through, and think Natas might just go for it. He's more concerned about your broader potential. In exchange, he agrees to leave you and us alone. I mean, why not agree to limit your calling to those who you really care about and minister to? You just said you believe six billion people or eighty-six percent of the population won't make it anyway."

"Dad, are you serious?"

"If Natas would agree to this, but you don't, you'd be risking a lot. You know what *these people* are capable of."

"What about all those other people I might have otherwise saved? How do I look my Savior in the eye?" Jak put his face in his hands and for the first time since this madness started, I saw him teary-eyed. He appeared weary and tired now, like the stress was finally wearing on him. That made two of us.

"Jak, I actually want to have Cherokee suggest that Natas propose this to you, not you to him."

"What?"

"I know that if you can plant an idea, a plan, in someone's mind as their own idea, they are a thousand times more likely to support it. If we can get him to support it and propose it to you, you take it. But not in your heart, Son. We'll bluff. But if you save him, we'll still win. It buys us time—maybe a year or so depending on how fast you grow your congregation. But, of course, you'll have to at least temporarily dial down your social media serving, and plans for televangelism. No mass ministry during this time. Natas will invite you to try to save him. If you do within a year, all limits on your calling will be removed."

Jak was clearly now overwhelmed, and needed a timeout. The grin was gone, but he got grounded.

"I need to finish up my message for tomorrow, Dad."

"Okay. I'm sorry to hit you with this as you prepare your Palm Sunday and Easter messages. I'll head over to your place. But like you said, please think about it."

"I will, Dad. I'm up to this, and I am on board with your plan, or God's plan, however it turns out."

God had a plan all right.

10

I left the church and walked over to Jak's and settled into a recliner on the porch. I had just relaxed with Goldie, who was hoping I had some food, and was startled by Eileen calling.

"Hello, Eileen. What's up?"

"Hi, Rob. I have Kraig Nelson on the line with us."

"Kraig, how you doing, buddy?"

"Great, Rob. I'm glad we caught you. Sorry to call on Saturday, but do you have a few minutes?"

"Of course. Is it in regards to the draft asset purchase agreement I did for that Missouri acquisition?"

Kraig's company, Heartland Desires XX, LLC, owns and operates sixty-nine adult bookstores mostly in the midwest and southwest areas. They are highly regulated by the various local jurisdictions, but you can see a lot of them along the interstate. Kraig was negotiating with the owner of ten such locations operating under the name of "XXX Show Me State of Mind" along Interstate 70 between St. Louis and Columbia, Missouri. Kraig's business model involved leasing some of the assets, including the real estate. XXX owns their properties, and was proposing to lease them to Kraig and sell him the business assets.

"Yeah, I heard back from Peter Richards, the guy who owns XXX who I briefly told you about last week. He has not engaged his lawyer yet to go over the purchase agreement to save legal fees. He's turned off by attorneys, but said he did not want to agree to the escrow or his personal guarantee," Kraig explained.

I had helped Kraig, like many other clients, grow his business through acquisitions and by purchasing competitive businesses. I maintain that when representing a buyer, it is very important to have some protections against the seller post-closing in case some of the representations, warranties, and agreements they make during the deal turn out to be less than accurate or as advertised. As in courtship, business deals sometimes get screwed up.

"Well, Kraig, as you know, you need some form of protection going forward. I mean, what if some of his videos violate copyrights, a condom leaks, or he doesn't have the proper local permits and licenses, or if some of his locations allow the patrons to score more than is legally allowed?"

"I know, but Richards is hell-bent against a personal guarantee, and claims he can't escrow any money. He says his selling corporation is fully leveraged, and after payment to creditors and vendors there will be no cash left for escrow."

"That's even more reason to get some protection in case some of these issues and liabilities conceived on his watch give birth on yours."

I could hear Eileen chuckle on our conference call.

"Funny, Rob, but Peter's attitude has hardened on this issue."

"You told me he was otherwise quite wealthy, right?"

"Oh, yeah. His online adult toy business is spurting out cash like crazy. But I know where you are going. I already asked if he could have that business guarantee our deal, and he adamantly declined."

"Okay, but you also said that he owns the real estate for these XXX locations and was going to lease them to Heartland, right? If any issues arise, you could simply not pay him rent."

"Yes, but I also already asked him if he would agree to lease rent setoff rights and, again, he declined."

"So you already exhausted our three normal forms of protection—our corporate prophylactics—the escrow, the personal guarantee, and lease setoff rights?"

"Yes, and strike three."

"What about a letter of credit? Did you ask him for that?"

"Yup, strike four."

"Does he have any children?" I should have been focusing on Jak's situation, but I also had to help clients or I'd lose them. Kraig needed cover if he was going to do this deal. Richards's real estate might be the resolution.

"What?"

"Just kidding, but do you know if his real estate for these Missouri locations is encumbered?"

"Not sure I see the relevance, Rob, but if you are thinking about a second lien or something, strike five. I discussed that with Richards, and although he said there were nominal mortgages on the properties, he would not give us a second lien against that equity."

"Kraig, how badly are you attracted to these assets?"

"Which ones?"

"Funny, but you know what I mean, some assets you just do not touch unless you have protection."

"Seriously, these locations would allow me to fully penetrate that I-70 corridor, and I would have virtually no competition. I've already got Kansas City to Columbia covered pretty well, but I'm bare between Columbia and St. Louis. Those stores I covet currently spew out almost a million dollars of profit per year, and under the Heartland operating model, I think we can double that in no time. The purchase price multiple Richards has agreed to is only one point eight on the Heartland pro forma basis. Therefore, this deal is attractive—not only strategically, but financially."

"All right, are there any other major issues you know of so far with Richards?"

"He said he went through the draft purchase agreement and no other issues popped out, and I get the idea this is the big one."

"All right, here's the deal, go back to Richards and tell him that you will proceed with the purchase if we can put in the asset purchase agreement and the leases with his entity that owns the real estate, and that they agree not to encumber any of the real estate with any additional debt so that you are always assured that there is at least fifty percent equity in the locations. They also agree not to sell the real estate or transfer the leases for a period of two years. As you know, most issues bare themselves within the first few months of a deal anyway so if he agrees to this, which he should, you should have adequate protection."

"Hmm, I really like that idea, Rob. Can I pay for your advice with some gift certificates from Heartland XX?"

"Hell no, Kraig. Now drop off and call Richards."

"Thanks, but your partner, Jim, gladly took some certificates..."

Click.

As I suspected. Jim and I need to talk.

"Eileen, you still on?"

"Sure, I was kind of enjoying the exchange, and, once again, a satisfied client."

"Eileen, the addresses for the XXX locations Kraig wants to buy and lease are listed on Exhibit A to the draft asset purchase agreement. I know it's Saturday, but can you go online to the appropriate State of Missouri County Register of Deeds offices? Verify exactly who owns the real estate and who holds any mortgages or liens, the amounts thereof, and the assessed values. If we are going to go this route, we need to be extra thorough in our due diligence."

"Got it. I'm on it."

"Thanks, Eileen."

"Bye."

Jak was finishing up a phone call while walking over from the church. "Okay, see you in a few minutes."

"Who's on the way?"

"Stan. He picked up my mike at the office and just finished casing the park. He'll be here shortly. He also described his proposal for my contingent fee arrangement. It's quite creative, Dad."

"What is it?"

"Well, Stan sounded pretty proud of his idea, and I think he wants to explain it to you himself."

"I can't wait." I smirked and rolled my eyes. Perhaps my pessimism was perceptible.

Jak grinned, his optimism was obvious.

Shelly came out and joined us on the porch. "I'm going to the store. You guys need anything?"

I got out my wallet and handed her a twenty dollar bill. Can you get me and Stan another 12 pack of Colt 45s? And keep the change, you filthy animal."

"Nice, Rob, so *Home Alone*."

"Yep."

"I think I'll go with my wife," said Jak. He placed his arm around Shelly's shoulders and she smiled up at him. Ah, young love.

"Okay, I'll hang out. It's great out here, I'll catch up on office work."

"We'll just be gone a few, Dad."

I was in the porch recliner and had March Madness on again. It was Sweet 16 weekend, one of my favorites. Mother Nature had turned the thermostat down to a most comfortable seventy-nine degrees, a slight new breeze was gently ruffling the leaves, flower petals, porch chimes, and Goldie's fur. I had grabbed some potato chips, and she wanted me to share. I did. Another satisfied canine companion.

I deleted a bunch of spam and responded to a few emails, drafted some documents and sent them to a couple clients.

Gotta pay the bills. Then I decided there was something I needed to do, even if I didn't really want to.

You know how most days there seems to be a thing or two you know you should do, but you really don't want to? We often get conflicting signals and let things get in the way to prevent us from doing what we should. Maybe sometime it involves a subtle satanic influence stopping us. It had been a few weeks since I saw her, and a few days since I called her. I get depressed when I do, and I get depressed when I don't. Her health is bad, and she can be difficult to understand, but she loves it when I visit or call. I knew I should call.

"Hello?"

"Hi, Mom. It's Rob."

"Hi, dear. I have not heard from you for a while."

"Yeah. Sorry. I've been in Atlanta."

"Oh, how's Jak doing?"

"He's fine for now, but I'm here helping a client." Hey, it was the truth. "How's your health, Mom?"

"Oh, about the same. My knees, hip, and ankles are always aching, but I still manage to get around the facility with my walker. These people help me with my meds and meals. But when are you coming to take me home?"

She almost always asks.

"Mom, you know you can't. I can't. You need assisted living." Although, I wished I could.

"But I get so lonely, and depressed, and I miss my dogs. I miss driving. I miss you. I miss your dad. I miss yesteryear, I miss everything." She was doing her best not to let me know she was crying.

Dad had died a decade ago, and I missed him, too. These calls reminded me of that too. I remember the day my dear dad died, though I kind of wish I didn't. He was one of my best friends, and my father. He did live until he was seventy-two, about average, I guess. But I was still saddened by his passing. I mean you only bury your dad once. But that's only literally speaking. Part of my lingering sadness was attributed to something somewhat selfish. I was in part sad for me for I would hurt, and miss the great times I had with my dad and friend. We would often go to Vegas, sometimes just me and Dad. We always won. But I still bury him in some ways.

It wasn't always this way. Not until I matured and realized Dad had been right about a lot of things I saw differently, albeit wrongly. He became my best friend only after I outgrew my stubborn idea that I had all the answers. I found out I didn't even understand all the questions. Neither did Dad, but he never pretended to.

He actually lived a pretty full and solid life, but his death, my best friend's funeral, was one of the saddest days of my life, so far.

"I know Mom, and I share some of your feelings. I'll try to do a better job of visiting and calling you."

"When?"

"I'll come see you when I get back in town later next week."

"Okay, I'm sorry." I could just see her wiping her tears and her eyes. Mine were moist, too. She did sound depressed and lonely. And now I was feeling very bad. Guilty. Mom lives in an assisted living facility in Omaha about twenty minutes from our house, and some weeks I do not even visit her. I also felt fear of my own future. Would I be on the other end of such a call some day?

"Don't be sorry, Mom. Hey, I'll bring you some chocolates."

"Okay."

"I've got another call coming. I'll see you next week, Mom. Love you."

"You, too. Bye."

At least I called.

An old friend really was calling—a long-time client as well. He owns Richard B. Long Holdings, a conglomerate of several companies.

"Hi, Dick. How ya doing?"

"Great, Rob. Sorry about your Bluejays losing last night, but they had a good year."

"They did. And we should be even better next season."

"Sounds like it. Hey, before I forget, thanks again for the game tickets and dinner a few weeks ago. Mary and I had a great time."

One of our family traditions is to go to the Arch Madness each spring for the Missouri Valley Conference basketball tournament in St. Louis. Recently we took Dick and his wife to one of Creighton's games and out to dinner. They live in St. Charles, a St. Louis suburb. It's nice, and prudent, to treat your clients once in a while. But I did not even submit an expense reimbursement to the firm, as I consider Dick a friend first, and a client a distant second.

"We did too, and you're very welcome."

"Remember the potential sale of my truck stops and the repair division I was telling you about? In fact, you drafted the letter of intent to get the deal started."

Dick's Holding Company owned a semi-truck repair business and truck stops operating three large facilities— two along I-70 in Missouri, and one on I-80 in Iowa. Millions of semi-trucks travel these interstates each year, and Dick's businesses are centrally located in the middle of the country, perfectly situated to help *keep 'em rolling*.

"Sure. You reach a firm deal yet?"

"We have, so I need you to convert that LOI you prepared into a binding asset purchase agreement. I think the only change is the price. We did some horse trading on some things, and I agreed to reduce the purchase price to seventeen point two million."

"At that price it must include your truck stops, too?"

"Yep."

"Okay, but Dick, since you do not own the real estate, the deal as proposed provides that you will assign the leases to the buyer. Will the landlords release your Holding Company from the leases and cancel your personal guarantees?"

"No. I asked but they all said no, so I'll have to rely on the buyer to perform under the leases."

"Do you know if the rents are market?"

"Oh, they are below market. I have good lease terms, which you helped me with fifteen years ago. The increase in value of these properties has greatly outpaced the small rent escalators you negotiated."

"I suspected as much. Since you are going to remain on the hook due to your guarantees anyway, why not keep your leases with the existing landlords, and sublease to the buyer? That way you keep some control over the locations and you can monitor the buyer's rent payments, and if he defaults, it'll be a lot easier for you to step back in since you'll already have your prime leases in place."

"Makes sense, but it sounds like a hassle to stay in the middle, collect rent from the buyer, and just hand it over to the landlords."

"Ah, but not if we make it worth your while. The rents are below market, so let's mark them up so you can keep a premium. You charge the buyer under the subleases "X" plus five thousand per month, but you only pay the landlords "X" each month. Worth the hassle?"

"Great idea, Rob. Draw up the papers that way."

There was another issue I wanted to address. Some of the large truck engine jobs can take several days and can cost ten to fifteen thousand dollars. Most customers paid when the repair or maintenance was completed and they picked up the truck. There was a concern I had discussed with Dick about how he was going to handle jobs that overlapped the closing date—jobs involving work commenced and parts purchased by Dick and his crew, but finished by the buyer, who would then collect from the customer after the deal closed.

"Okay. One other thing, Dick. How should we address the overlapping jobs we discussed?"

"Easy. Once we get a closing date set, I will make all the customers pre-pay the estimate up front, so I'll have all the money, and then after closing the buyer can finish the jobs."

"Richard, Richard, Richard. First, the buyer's probably not that stupid, but more importantly, you know dang well that I would not be any part of such a scheme. I'll provide in the agreement that as part of the inventory, you and the buyer will agree on an equitable proration of the jobs pending at closing. For the portion of the work you have completed, the buyer will pay you your share as an additional purchase price. Then he can collect from the customer and keep it all. Besides, that way we shift all of the collection risk to the buyer."

"Sounds good. I had to try."

Poor Rich. "No, you didn't. Anyway, I'll draft the docs for your review. Anything else, Dick?"

"Umm, yes, there is. Um, my financials include some miscellaneous income, part of which comes from inflated condom sales at the three truck stops."

"What?"

"Well, we have condom machines in the women's restrooms, too, but we keep them empty. The prostitutes put dollars in but get nothing out. The hookers hardly ever complain, since their purchase is evidence of their illegal intentions. So it's like one hundred percent profit."

"Dick, you've got to be kidding me!"

"Um, no. But I was up-front with the buyer and explained it to him. He said he's not going to continue the practice, so he wants to reduce the purchase price a little more. What should I do?"

"Easy Dick. Cease the shenanigans yourself ASAP. Either pull the vending machines out of the ladies' rooms or put condoms in them. And reduce the price. The buyer's right. You should even think about giving away some free condoms to make it right. On second thought, don't."

"Okay, Rob. I don't always like your advice from a bottom-line point of view, but it's hard to argue with your logic and ethics, or your moral compass. Besides, net net, anything I *lose* by you steering me to do the right thing is usually outweighed by the great legal and business advice you otherwise give me."

"Thanks Dick, anything else?"

"No. But I am going to be meeting with our mutual friend, Kraig Nelson. I hear he has you working on a deal as well."

"Yeah. Tell Kraig hello."

"I will. He wants me to mystery shop some of his XX stores for him. I also offered to do the same on those ten XXX stores you guys are working on."

"Richard, Richard. Richard. Good bye, my friend."

I almost took a nap right then and there on the porch recliner. Maybe I did. I was awakened by Jak, Shelly, and Stan. They pulled in the driveway simultaneously. I took a quick look at March Madness. Another fantastic finish. Shelly and Jak had some groceries, including my twelve-pack.

"Hey all, good to see you. Let me help you with that Shelly. I'll have a cold one. And guess what? Bradley just knocked off Kentucky on a buzzer beater. It was at the Louisville regional, so the fans were stunned because KU had virtually a home game, but the Braves pulled it off."

Another David beating Goliath.

"No way!" Jak exclaimed.

"Oh yeah, the madness marches on," I joked.

They all went inside to unload provisions. I continued working and following the Madness.

Eventually, we all ended up again on the porch. Stan came out with a cold 45 and a fresh one for me. Jak had some lemonade, and I wasn't sure what Shelly had. Stan settled in and also noted the serenity and great weather and setting as he lit up a Camel, no filter.

"Hey, Rob, did Jak tell you about the special contingent fee arrangement I conjured up for him and the firm?"

Jak grinned, and shook his head.

"No, but has the firm agreed?"

"Not yet. I'll submit it Monday, but I'll get it approved. I even intend to help Jak make some modest progress payments to the firm to keep the accounting nerds at bay along the way. But, I must say, it must be one of the most creative, out-of-this-world contingent fee arrangements in the history of the legal profession," Stan boasted.

I cocked my head toward Stan and gave him a skeptical smirk. "The suspense is killing me."

"It *is* pretty cool, Dad."

"Jak, do you want to explain it, or should I?"

"Go ahead, Stan. It's your case, your idea."

"Okay, here goes. It's basically an all-or-nothing proposition. Jak says I'm a work in progress, but tomorrow he is baptizing me. I guess there are five of us are being baptized on Palm Sunday. We're ready to accept Jesus as our Savior, and try our best to walk with him."

"Stan, that's fantastic. But how does this relate to Jak's deal with the firm?" I interrupted.

"As you know, I've done very well at the firm and with no kids to support, I've built a small fortune. I can help Jak and even guarantee his account with the firm. Heck, he's like the son I never had. Anyway, if Jak helps me be saved, and I am part of the eternal Kingdom, I will personally pay the firm whatever Jak owes. If I am *not* saved when Jesus returns, Jak owes the firm nothing."

Jak was grinning.

I looked at Stan with severe skepticism, head tilted and eyebrows lowered. "But Stan, we won't know whether you are saved until Jesus comes again, at which time all legal bills will become irrelevant."

"Exactly!"

"Okay, but Jak, how will you keep Stan in line to be saved?"

Jak explained, "Well, it's not just Stan, but all of us need to remain vigilant and saved. You see, God gives us many blessings to try to keep us in line, including the ultimate promise of His Kingdom if we choose to walk with His Son. Those blessings include things like family, fellowship, friends, church, the Bible, dogs and butterflies, wonders like the Grand Canyon, Montana, sunsets, peace, comfort, courage, faith, love and hope, mom and dad, and apple pie…"

"And don't forget children," I interrupted.

"And sex, too," Stan added.

"Good one, Stan," I said as I brushed him off.

"Actually Dad, Stan is kinda right. God gives us the choice and ability to love others, as well as Him and His Son. But I think you get the point."

Stan and I nodded as Jak continued.

"Staying on the path with Jesus would be a lot easier if these blessings dominated our lives. But we remain vulnerable until we die, or Jesus returns. We remain vulnerable to the many tools Satan has in his tool box, as he tries to make us question God. He sometimes uses indirect forces to weaken us, like loss of a job or loved one, cancer, accidents, crime, bad weather or luck, envy, old age, war, terrorism, and the like. He can attack us through real people, like *these people*, but he also attacks us with things like temptation, greed, pride, addiction, sloth, love of money, hatred, selfishness, and the list goes on. I call these Satan's sin attractants."

Shelly stayed silent and shifted in her seat. I guess she liked discussion of blessings much more than sin, but who could blame her? Sin was around us every day, and it was a war we were always waging.

"The on-going battle between good and evil?" I asked.

"That's right, Dad, and all of us are right in the midst of it every day as we try to resist Satan's attempts to draw us to sin with his bag of lies, and away from Jesus."

"Even if we have been saved at one point in time and have accepted Jesus Christ as our Savior, 'saved for now' if you will, we remain vulnerable, and can become un-saved at any point until we die or Jesus returns."

Shelly now spoke. "I have struggled with that concept ever since it was first explained to me. I mean, every night when we go to bed, should we look back on every one of our daily thoughts and actions and ask ourselves if we are still saved? That seems ridiculous."

"Actually, dear, that would not be a bad exercise, but I don't think it is necessary. Most days we will make some type of mistake or trip up along the path, but if we keep the faith and Jesus in our hearts, our shortcomings are forgiven by God's grace, our sins are washed away with Jesus's sacrifice for us."

Stan stood up and paced the porch with another Camel. He, too, had a good question.

"So Jak, you're telling me that if my record is clean, I live a good life, give to the poor, don't harm anyone, have no vices, et cetera, but I have not accepted Jesus as my Savior, then I will not be saved?"

"That's right."

"So our actions do not matter?" Stan sat back down after he posed this question. I think we all knew the answer Jak would give.

"Of course they do. If you truly accept Jesus in your heart you will want to live a godly life. Being saved does not depend on our actions though, as it depends on our faith and keeping Jesus in our hearts."

I shifted in the porch recliner, removed my glasses and scratched my head. "If we are saved and have accepted Jesus, we can lose it?"

"Yes, Dad. Many Bible verses discuss or allude to this very concept." Jak continued by quoting some Scripture.

'And you will be hated by all for My name's sake. But he who endures to the end will be saved.'

— Matthew 10:22

'But the ones on the rock are those who, when they hear, received the word with joy, and these have no root, who believe for a while and in time of temptation fell away.'

— Luke 8:13

'Strengthening the souls of the disciples, exhorting them to continue in the faith, and saying "We must through many tribulations enter the Kindgom of God."'

— Acts 14:22

"But Jak, if this is all true, since no one is perfect and we all sin once in a while, do we constantly move back and forth between being saved and un-saved?" Stan asked.

"No, I don't think so. True, we often make daily choices between right and wrong—some right, some wrong. And the line between good and evil is often blurred or even drawn differently from one person to the next. We stumble and sway sometimes. But to be saved and sustain it, you must avoid a *life* of sin. There is a huge difference between a life of sin, and people who sin. Children of God who walk steadfastly through life with Jesus in their heart, despite periodic shortcomings and sin, will be saved. Children of Satan, who live a life of sin and have not accepted Jesus as the Son of God, our Savior, will not be."

"I understand, I think."

A fine line indeed. Jak's landline started ringing, and he and Shelly went inside.

I think Stan and I both took some comfort knowing that some of our faults and sins could be overlooked. I know I fail to live a godly life sometimes, and even feel like I've let Jesus out of my heart. It can be the worst feeling ever.

11

S tan and I were still out on the porch as the sun was beginning its descent and another Earthly day was approaching its finality. We had fresh, cold Colt 45s, and Stan lit another Camel, no filter. The breeze gave me a small waft of second-hand carcinogens. I resisted the urge to cough, and took a swig instead. Stan inhaled deeply, and reclined back quite comfortably. I had turned the TV on to more March Madness, and I saw through the picture window that some cream was rising to the top today. Duke and Kansas both advanced—some rhyme and reason within the madness.

Jak and Shelly again joined us.

"We just ordered a couple different kinds of pizzas, guys. They should be here in thirty minutes," Jak informed us.

"Sounds great," Stan and I said in a synchronized voice.

"So, Jak, you ready for your message tomorrow?" I asked.

"Yep." He wore weathered jeans, two t-shirts, and a determined expression.

"I can't wait to hear it, Jak. It will be the first time I get to hear you perform as a pastor."

He grinned.

"Stan, did you get Jak's mike for his meeting with Natas?" I wanted to work on the meeting. It unnerved me a bit to think of my son dealing one-on-one with the leader of the Dark Angels, and though I trusted that Jak could handle it, I wanted to make sure every detail was right to ensure our success.

"I did. Pretty simple. We can hear him and Natas, but we can't communicate to him. That'd be too obvious."

"What about the park? Did you case it?"

"I did. We can have Homeless Dan situated close to the meeting spot, and he'll get there a little early."

"Perfect," I said. "What about us? Where can we watch and listen?"

"There's a walkway, a boardwalk type area, above the lagoon that usually has people on it where we can blend in and have a good view."

"Okay. I think we need to get some pencil and paper and map out the area," I said.

We did. Mapping out the logistics would prove to be the easy part.

"We've got company," Stan announced a bit later.

A vanilla sedan pulled up.

"That doesn't look like the pizza guy," Jak said.

They parked in front of the porch, and we all recognized Officers Crow and Tuey, though they had someone else with them. This time they had an unmarked car.

"I guess you missed me, huh, Crow?" Stan asked.

"Enough of your crap, Manilow. Why didn't you help us with the photo and that church? Why did your now dead ex-client have a photo of that church, right across from this place?"

"First Crow, who is your new sidekick?"

"I'll ask the questions, Manilow, but meet our department's new Public Relations partner, Aimee Cunningham. She's with Channel 6."

"Why the media?" I chimed in.

"I'll ask the questions," Crow stated without really looking at me. "She's off the record for now, but if we have a story here, something I can solve, it might help my run for Fulton County Sheriff," Crow explained.

"Frankly, Crow," said Stan rather glibly while combing his hair. "When you showed us the photo we were surprised you and Tuey did not say you came to us because of it. I mean, it's so obvious. Did you really need our help to connect the dots? A six-year-old's dot-to-dot book might be more challenging."

"Okay, Manilow, we missed one, but now we know that your buddy here, Rob Ross, rented a car that made the ten o'clock news. Exploded before it could be stolen. A witness saw it near Gil Egan's murder scene. Coincidence?"

"No, and if we're off the record, we might be able to help you with your political aspirations, as well as your media partner. We think there *is* a connection between Gil's death and Jak's church."

"Okay, Manilow. Continue." Seeing that we might be of assistance to his lofty goals, Crow now allowed Stan to talk.

"It's a complex story, but Egan was part of a bad group of anti-Christians trying to get Jak to stop his ministry. Their Holding Company is technically the Dark Angels Limited Family Partnership, but I don't know much about them yet. We think they asked Gil to kill Rob before he got here to help Jak. We also think they are responsible for blowing up Rob's rental."

"So Rob killed Gil instead?" Crow offered.

"Of course not," Stan corrected. "God knows who really killed Egan, it could have been self-defense for all we know. But Jak does have a meeting scheduled with *these people* on Wednesday. If you give us until then to work through this, we agree to give you a full report and all the credit for a thorough investigation, and an exclusive to your media partner."

Aimee finally spoke "Care if I ask some questions, Detective?"

"Go ahead," Crow agreed.

"Who is Rob Ross?"

"I'm Jak's dad. Jak is the church pastor," I said as I pointed to the church. "I'm here to help Jak, as is Stan, er, Manilow."

She looked at me and studied me for a moment. "Detective Crow, the other photo. Let's see it. I think it's a picture of Mr. Ross here."

Crow pulled out the other blood-stained photo of me.

"It sure as hell is. Why didn't you guys...oh, never mind." He stopped because he was embarrassed enough.

"Like I said, I am pretty sure Gil Egan was on a mission to kill Rob," Stan repeated.

"Okay," Aimee continued.

"So have *these people* made threats?" she asked.

"Oh, yeah," I confirmed. "They threatened the former pastors here and their families, and now Jak."

"Have they followed through on any threats?" she inquired.

"We think so," I responded. "Clearly they have by trying to kill me, but it is often hard to tell if our setbacks are caused by *these people* or just circumstance."

"How do you mean?"

"Well ma'am, as an example, Jak told us that about a week ago they sent him an untraceable text threatening to do hardship to his wife." I nodded toward Shelly. "The very next day as she was walking to work a man tried to steal her purse. Some kind pedestrians pursued him and the thief dropped the purse. So she got it back, but he got away. He did not want that purse. But *these people* successfully scared the hell out of Shelly, and sent Jak a clear message. It was clearly the work of *these people,* but the other setbacks we suffer are more subtle."

"So why have you not contacted us?" Crow questioned.

"They told us it would get worse if we did," Stan explained and bit back an opportunity to really embarrass Crow.

"Do you know where they are located?"

"No," Stan said too quickly.

"Yes, we actually do," I corrected.

Eileen had done some more research for me. She, of course, used some of the technology that I detest.

"*These people* have an office in the Heller Federal Bank Building and front a presumably legitimate business called Psychic Dark Angels."

"What do they do?"

"Well, Detective Crow, believe it or not, for a fee, you can choose from a variety of services, such as palm reading, card reading, fortune telling, deeper meaning beyond your horoscope, and the like. You can stop by, but most of their services are delivered on the phone or online. They use sophisticated audio and video equipment to read palms and minds, even over the Internet. And, get this, again for a fee, they will purportedly cast a spell or curse on your enemy, adversary, opponent, or anyone you tell them to. For five thousand bucks you can name two recipients of their dreaded curse. They guarantee your targets will experience bad results within a week, or your money back. For ten thousand bucks, even worse results are guaranteed."

"My gosh, these can't all be legal can they?" Aimee asked.

"Well, I'm not sure they are breaking any laws. Are they Detective?" I looked toward both Crow and Sergeant Tuey, although the good Sergeant must have a daily word limit.

"I don't know. Depends on how they bring about the *results*, but I've never heard of them," Crow answered.

"They don't do a lot of advertising or promo activities," I explained. "They target receptive consumers through email and their website for the most part. They know who to market to through sophisticated research and digital device data. But remember, this business is really just their front."

"So Ross, what about the illegal activities you allege, like using Gil Egan, the threats, chasing away the former pastors, purse snatching, et cetera?" Crow inquired.

"That's all back behind the front. They know better than to do those things up front so they do most of the illegal activities behind the scenes."

"Hmm," pondered both Tuey and Crow.

"So when and where is this meeting?" Crow asked.

"It is…"

"All we can share now is that it is Wednesday," Stan quickly interrupted me, although it had not been confirmed yet with Natas.

"So we'll hear from you sometime Wednesday, right?"

"Sure. Exclusively." Stan looked toward Aimee.

"In the meantime, call if anything comes up or if you need our help." Detective Crow turned on his heel and the other two followed him.

"Right," Stan said to their retreating backs.

"What do you think, Stan?"

"I think Fulton County needs a new sheriff all right, but these guys are bad for the job. I mean, they did not ask Jak a single question, or even ask all of us where we were yesterday when Egan was killed, and the photo of you escaped them twice, until the reporter made the connection for them."

"But at least we can call them if we need their help," I offered wryly.

"Now *this* is the pizza guy," Jak announced as a small two-door sedan with an over large *Emo's Pizza* sign on its roof pulled in. A young lad carried two large half and half pies, breadsticks, and a forty dollar invoice to the porch. I handed him a Ben Franklin and told him to keep the change. It made his night—I like to do that once in a while, make someone's night or day. I often give Eileen extra compliments on her work as I know it encourages her and brightens her day just a little. But, it makes me feel good, too. So I guess, given the benefits bestowed back to me, it's not all that benevolent is it?

We settled in on the porch as Shelly brought out some paper plates and stuff. I grabbed a couple combo pieces, and went to the recliner. Best view into March Madness. Looked like Florida was about to punch a Sweet 16 ticket. It looked like the favored teams were winning and only a few underdogs were pulling off upsets. Chalk.

And guess who perched herself right by me? Yes, Goldie. She was hoping I would share some toppings or some crust. I did.

"So, Jak, what time is church tomorrow anyway?" I mumbled with some of Emo's still in my mouth.

"Well, tomorrow I have to go over early and set up the baptismal. It takes about twenty minutes to fill up with water, then it needs to sit a couple of hours to warm up. Then, I'll get ready for Sunday School at 10:00, and the Service is at 11:00."

"Sounds great, we'll then have lunch with Cherokee, and Shelly and I will go back to Omaha. Then I'll come back for the meeting with Natas. Let's eat and then work more on that meeting."

We went over the map we sketched out and our plan was coming together. It was getting late and Stan went over to the associate pastor's place, Jak and Shelly went upstairs, and I stayed on the porch with Goldie. I agreed to take the pizza boxes and garbage over to the church's dumpster, but I placed a piece of someone's crust on a window ledge. Goldie would enjoy it later.

I spent about another hour on the porch. Alone, I thought.

March Madness was wrapping up for the day, and so was I, but I had half a Colt 45 left, so I stayed on the porch. Another nice evening, albeit a bit overcast with no moon or visible stars. It was fairly dark, especially with no working street light. I thought I heard some footsteps a couple houses up, and sure enough, they were slowly getting closer. No big deal, someone out for a walk, but I got nervous when they turned on the sidewalk towards Jak's porch. Goldie also sensed something and scooted over next to me. Just who's supposed to be protecting whom here? The figure stopped about thirty feet way. All I could make out was the dark silhouette of what I figured was a mid-sized man.

"Can I help you?" I asked.

"Perhaps. Are you the boy's father?" he asked softly.

"Jak? Yeah. I'm Jak's dad."

"We heard you were here. I come in peace tonight, but I bring two messages. First, I live a block down the street and the boy left fliers and knocked at our door wanting to preach I presume. Please tell him to leave us alone."

"Are you affiliated with something else?"

"No comment. I am a neighbor who wants to be left alone. But, secondly, I bring you a heads-up to prove our people mean business and will take extreme measures."

Oh crap. All of the sudden the warm air turned ice cold.

"Do you know one of the preacher's young followers, a kid named Jay Jay?"

"No, I do not."

"Well, you will. Some harm may be coming his way. Have a pleasant evening."

The figure left.

I was calmly overwhelmed. Oh my God. After nearly being killed, my rental car blown up, Stan shot and Jak and Shelly threatened, I realized that *these people* have probably been in our lives in varying degrees forever. The realization that *these people* were actually organized in some sects scared the hell out of me. For most people, *these people* are on the fringe and periphery. But for us, they were now very real and blunt.

As I thought about it, *these people* come and go like fleeting moments, or thoughts. They probably always have. Think back in your life, as far back as you can. The seemingly random bad breaks when things did not go your way, or you made the wrong choice or decision. Did *you* not do the right thing? Were *you* solely responsible for the poor decisions and things you are not proud of? Lousy luck and lewd lust. Things you want to forget but will probably always remember, like times when greed arm wrestled with generosity and greed won hands down. When your vice was victorious over virtue, times when temptation tangled with the Ten Commandments and Moses tumbled. When our discipline was detoured by desire, times when kindness went toe-to-toe with rudeness and kind of got the boot. Occasions when we needed to be tough as nails, but our weakness got our integrity hammered, when our selfishness went head-to-head with service to others, and the others took it on the chin. Times when doing the right thing was not the convenient thing. When we gave up or gave in. I can think of many such times in my life. Were *these people* with me?

Are these lifetime low periods really random and matters of pure circumstance? Are they really the result of our own shortcomings, or are there things and people on our peripheral existence nudging us off the path, albeit less than forthcoming? Is there some lower, darker spirit at work in our lives? I believe in the Holy Spirit, and how good things can happen to us, often through real people, or angels. But what about the flip side? Do sin and evil surround us and influence us through real people?

These people proved that they indeed do.

Just who the hell are *these people*?

Now what do I do?

We actually face that question a lot, now don't we? I decided to see if Jak was still awake. If I kept this to myself and something happens to Jay Jay, no one would believe me. They would say I had one-too-many Colt 45s, or I saw a ghost. They might be half right. I went inside with Goldie and quietly went up the stairs. Jak's door was cracked and a soft light was on. He was reading.

"Jak," I whispered.

He got up and came out into the hall.

"Shh. Shelly's sleeping. What's up?"

"Do you have a minute?"

"Yeah, come here. Let's go into the den."

He turned on a lamp. "Dad, you look pale and you're, like, shaking. That's not like you. Did you see a ghost?" I wished he was half wrong.

"Jak, some man approached me on the porch. He kept his distance in the dark and I could not recognize him. All I know is he said he's a neighbor, and I think he's with *these people*. I don't know if he was giving us a warning or trying to make a point by taking credit for something that has not yet happened."

"What?"

"Is there a Jay Jay in your congregation?"

"Yeah, he's Jon Anders's son. Why?"

"Who's John Anderson?"

"No. Jon Anders. He's on our church board, owns a sign shop, and races stock cars on the side. Jay Jay is Alisa and Jon Anders's son."

"Jak, this man in the dark told me that some harm may be coming Jay Jay's way."

"Dang, now what do we do?" Jak wondered, and looked out a window into darkness.

"Do Jon and Alisa know about *these people*?"

"Oh, yeah. They and others in the congregation are concerned that I will also cave in to *these people* and stop leading the church, like their prior pastors did."

"Jak, I think, I think we need to give Jon and Alisa a heads-up on this. Not sure there is much we or they can do. But I think we need to. How old is Jay Jay anyway?"

"He's nineteen and goes to the local college and lives at home. Good kid. He's in our Youth Group."

"Okay, do you want to talk to the Anders, Jak?"

"Sure. I'll see them in the morning at Sunday School."

"Okay, just let me know if they want to talk to me. I'm gonna go back downstairs and check-in for the night."

"Did you lock the door?"

"Yeah, and Goldie came inside, too. Night."

Damn, did we need prayers.

12

Sunday, March 23

It was early on Palm Sunday morning, and Jak was already over at the church. Shelly, Stan, and I were on the porch and had coffee and rolls to eat, and the paper to read. There's something soothing about reading the Sunday paper. Even the gloomy bad news goes down easier with some Sunday morning coffee.

Shelly went to Sunday School around 10:00 a.m., and Stan and I paid some more bills on the porch. Stan asked for my opinion on some of Cherokee's issues. I had some ideas for both her personally and her endorsement agreements, so I sent her some suggestions and copied Stan. She must work on Sunday, too, as I got a quick email reply: *Great ideas, Rob! See you in a few.*

Stan said his laptop was about out of juice, and asked how mine was. I was plugged into the only outlet on the porch, but had about ninety percent battery life left. So I unplugged mine and plugged in Stan's. Akin to scuba divers sharing oxygen from one good tube.

The phone rang and I saw that Eileen was calling.

"Hi there."

"Hi, Rob, I was just getting back to you on a couple of research projects."

"Great. Let's hear it."

"First, not much new on Cherokee other than what we already knew. It looks like she has scaled back on her social media activity. But, the Dark Angels' website claims she is a member. Her website neither confirms nor denies, but she has shared some very positive experiences with Pastor Jak Ross and the Eternal Life Church of God. I thought that was neat. But, other than that, not much else."

"Okay, good."

"I also did some deeper digging on the Dark Angels. Their world-wide leader is a bad guy named Natas". I knew some of this already, but let her go on. "Rob, *these people* are bad news. Natas has been compared to some devilish people. Let me read you what one website says about him.

'The dangerous Natas has been compared to the likes of other behind-the-scenes criminals, such as mafia leaders, drug lords, and brothel owners. Through his executive board, called the Sin Council, and other networks, he has orchestrated more criminal activity than any other lost soul currently on the planet. But, he remains elusive due to the lack of direct evidence that he personally has carried out any of his crimes. There is circumstantial evidence that he has directed and ordered the Dark Angels and their agents to carry out both grievous misdeeds and small subtle temptations, all in an attempt to sway or destroy Christians. But he continues to frustrate government authorities as well as Christian leaders. Some leading theologians claim that organizations such as the Dark Angels are largely responsible for society's shortcomings, such as adultery, crime, homelessness, and substance abuse. They are said to be the opposite of angels on earth.'

"I also found a reported case that turned my stomach and brought me to tears." She told me how Natas and his gang were having a hard time convincing a pastor to stop saving souls. So, instead of harming the pastor's wife or kids, Natas masterminded a heinous killing of their dog. The pastor's family had an adorable Collie called Ring. She was brown with a ring of white fur around her collar. While they were vacationing in Florida they left Ring at a nice kennel. Ring was one of the family and they struggled leaving her behind, but she could not go with them. At Natas's direction, *these people* went to the kennel and posed as friends of the family to pick up the dog and house her themselves, and the kennel screwed up and gave Ring to *these people*. They took Ring to a vacant lot out in the country, where Natas and a couple cronies were waiting to videotape what happened next. They had dug a hole about two feet deep and three of them tied her legs and forced a terrified Ring into the hole. The audio captured the whimpering as they buried the dog up to her ring of white fur with only her head and top shoulders above ground. Ring struggled to escape but her legs were tied. Her whimpering continued but could no longer be heard after Natas started the Lawn Boy. He approached Ring, tilted the mower up and mowed Ring to death. *These people* sent the video to the pastor's iPad with a message from the kennel that Ring was also enjoying the vacation. The pastor decided to open it and watch it with his family. Natas not only ruined their vacation, he ruined their lives. Counseling for the kids failed to prevent one of them from committing suicide. The pastor ended up quitting his calling.

I felt queasy and patted Goldie to help me calm down a bit. Eileen offered more heinous examples. "There's more, including additional specific atrocities they have implemented, do you want me to continue?"

"No, Eileen, I think I know who, or what, we are dealing with. Thanks, and thanks for calling on a Sunday. I gotta go." I tried to erase that video from my mind, and wanted to hug my dogs.

God, I thought, *am I glad there is one.*

The church parking lot was filling quickly, so Stan and I logged off and headed over.

"I'll hardly know anyone, and I suppose there is no way we will know who *these people* are, huh?" I asked Stan.

"I doubt it. They'll probably blend right in with the members and potential members."

"That makes sense," I added. "On the outside, it is hard to distinguish the good people from not so good sometimes." How true!

The gentlemanly neighbor who always smiles and waves could also be the habitual embezzler next door. Some people you just don't know—friend or foe?

Some greeters were on the church steps, and they knew Stan. He introduced me.

A nice elderly white-haired man approached me. "Welcome, Mr. Ross. I am Eddy Buchard, an elder here. We are pleased you can visit and be with us today, and we are *so* happy your son is our pastor. He's an incredible young man. We hope we can keep him, and that he keeps leading us."

"Thank you, Mr. Buchard. Me, too." At least I think.

We were still out on the church steps and patio meeting people when a black stretch limo pulled into the parking lot. I pulled Stan aside.

"*These people* wouldn't be so obvious to show up in a limo, would they?"

"No Rob, that's Cherokee. She does not drive."

The limo driver opened Cherokee's door, escorted the lovely, graceful woman to the sidewalk, and then drove away.

"C'mon Rob, I'll introduce you."

She had aged gracefully, if not naturally. Hardly a wrinkle and her long silky black hair still glimmered in the morning sun.

"My pleasure Cherokee," I said as I shook her soft hand, amazed with her presence. I took in her full-length black dress, dress shoes, bright, white pearl necklace, and her own brand handbag.

"Thanks, Rob. I've heard a lot about you, and I look forward to working with you."

I was not expecting that.

We proceeded into the church and exchanged numerous pleasantries and a few new introductions, as clearly some of *these people* were new or recent attendees. I followed Stan and Cherokee, assuming they had a favorite pew or general area in which to sit. They did, as do most.

I tried to scan the sanctuary without being obvious. It was almost full, there were probably over 150 people, and now I knew just a handful of them. It felt weird to be among a multitude of strangers who were looking to your son to lead them to the Kingdom. Did they really know what they were up against?

The organist stopped, and a deaconess who was sitting upfront with Jak approached the podium and made some announcements. Then Jak and three Youth Group members got guitars and microphones, and along with a piano player, led us in song. Jak plays guitar and piano, and his voice is such that he could do quite well with a touring Christian band if this gig flamed out.

A Scripture reading followed the singing and then a children's sermon. The children went up to the front and sat or knelt down. An elder explained in simple terms for the kids, as well as for the rest of us, the upcoming week including Good Friday and Jesus's resurrection on Easter. The kids were given little chocolate bunnies and returned to their pews and proud parents.

Jak picked up the offering plates, and asked the deacons and deaconesses to come forward for receiving His tithes and our offerings. After a brief prayer about our many blessings and thanks, he gave them the plates to pass through the pews. I heard idle chit-chat, small children, and normal church noise. I could hear several whispered conversations within the sanctuary. The peripheral noise and light clatter were such that I could only catch a few words and phrases from people unknown, but not enough to follow the lead. My sense of peripheral hearing remained blurred, but in a way, the common church noise sounded as familiar as my own breathing.

People were probing in their pockets, purses, and wallets. Stan was writing a check. I noticed Cherokee's was already done. It looked like one of those slightly over-sized pre-printed bank drafts. She folded it and held it in her lap as the plates were still a few pews away.

The organist softly played "The Joy of Our Faith" as background music and I sang along in my head *May the joy of our faith shine through....* It is one of my favorites.

I again scanned the audience for any clues or hints of our pretending visitors. Nothing, or no one really stood out amongst the multitudes. Funny how only God knows who we really are. Not even *we* know who we really are, let alone others.

The offering plates passed through our row and the checks and cash were piling high. As a visitor I was not expected to give, but I put that twenty dollar bill I found in the ATM in the plate as it passed by. There was the normal whisperings, sniffles, note passing, dull stares, head scratching, and fidgeting. No doubt some were praying, and others were thinking about their afternoon, week, or life ahead. Maybe even beyond.

The plates were returned to the front, and Jak placed them on the altar right by some burning candles and a large, open Bible.

The organist stopped, and Jak came to the front edge of the altar, on the top step, grinning.

"At this time would Knowa, Keagan, Stan, Ashter, and Marcus come forward, please." Marcus had been a long-time friend of mine back in Omaha who I could always count on, in many ways. Marcus and his wife, Deanne, had been our neighbors and favorite friends for what seemed like forever. They had followed Jak to Georgia, and Marcus wanted to formalize it.

They all went forward, and one by one, Jak put his hands on their shoulder. He asked each of them, "Do you accept Jesus Christ as your Savior, and do you believe he is the Son of God, died on the cross for us, and will return again to accept his followers into the Kingdom?"

They all affirmed. Jak addressed the congregation.

"Members of Eternal Life Church of God, do you pledge and agree to help these new members in Christ to stay on the path with Jesus?"

"We do!" the members responded in unison.

"At this time we also invite the families up to circle around the baptismal."

"Rob, come on," Shelly said softly. "Jak wants you and me to come to the front for Stan." I had wondered why Shelly was toting a terrycloth towel.

About thirty or so of us surrounded the baptismal font, a tub about three feet by six feet with about thirty-six inches of water in it.

One by one, they entered the water, and Jak fully immersed them, and baptized them. For each one he announced, "I now baptize you in the name of Jesus Christ for the remission of sins." It was pretty cool. When you think about it, what I do for my clients pales in comparison.

After we returned to our seats, we were asked to stay standing and again join in singing.

Jak and the newly baptized (and hopefully saved) members had left briefly to dry off and get dry clothes. As they returned, we were asked to sit.

It was time for Jak's message. He would actually deliver and throw out several messages, if we could only accept them. He approached the podium, that almost-always-present-grin beaming out inclusively to all. He put his Bible on the podium and became quite serious. Silence now dominated the congregation. My God, he looked so determined. The people in the congregation actually seemed like they were most eagerly awaiting Jak's message.

"Good morning, and welcome everybody. Thank you for coming. Let us pray.

"Lord, thank You for bringing all these people here today. Please help them receive and understand Your Word through my word. Thank You, Lord, for sending Your Son to come and save us from our sins and to give us the opportunity to receive eternal life. Please help these people here today to hear Your Word and accept Your Son as their Savior who can lead them to eternal salvation in Your Kingdom forever. Some souls are ready, some for now, and some souls are not. Some never will be. But that will always be the case, dear Lord. In any event, please send Your Son again to save us and lead us to Your Kingdom as soon as possible. Amen."

"Amen," the followers responded.

Jak began his sermon with a message about Palm Sunday.

He told us that Palm Sunday was the start of the week where God gave up His only Son for us, and that Jesus was willing to give His life to wash away our sins. Jak talked about the resurrection and how Jesus will come again. Our Savior was not only crucified, but He is coming again to save us! Easter should be Christians' most decorated and celebrated holiday. Because the single most important thing in our life is to be sure, that on Judgment Day, God knows us and we are accepted into the Kingdom. Jak concluded that portion of his Palm Sunday message.

He seemed to shift his sermon in the direction of both *these people* and his people. He paused, took a drink of water, and then continued his message.

"Imagine, if you can, that you were diagnosed with an incurable form of cancer, and given six to twelve months to live. Your life is turned upside down and you can barely bear it. You go through the various psychological phases of denial, anger, self-pity, and so on. You eventually accept it, and plan for a premature death as best you can praying for your soul. Your body and your days are dwindling and decaying. You literally feel life slowly exiting your existence. Only a few grains of sand are left in the top half of your hourglass. Then, one day your doctor explains there is this experimental, yet promising, new drug that could possibly treat your cancer. He suggests you try it, you do, and it miraculously works. Your life is saved, or at least for now. Your hourglass is turned upside down again. You're not sure if your prayers had been answered, since your prayers had turned from saving your life, to saving your soul. In any event, just a few weeks later you run into an old acquaintance you had lost contact with."

Jak was slowly pacing back and forth up on the altar and speaking into his mike. "Your long lost friend tells you about *his* terminal cancer, the same type of cancer and death penalty you had been given. You wonder whether you should tell him about the drug you were given that saved your life. Should you tell him and introduce him to your doctor? Would you?"

Jak stops at the podium, pauses, and speaks softly into his mike. "Of course you would." He paused again for a few moments and the silence was deafening. The people in the congregation were firmly fixated on Jak and his message and wanted more.

"Now, let me ask you this. If you had a chance to save someone's life—someone's soul—forever, would you do it? Some of you can probably see the connection between that life-saving drug and the introduction of your doctor to your old friend, and the acceptance of Jesus Christ into our hearts resulting in eternal salvation. A miracle drug plus a new doctor equals a life saved, for now. The sustained acceptance of Jesus Christ in a heart equals a soul saved, forever.

"Folks, this is not some fictional story or parable. It is very real, and should be happening in our lives. God's Word commands each one of us to reach out and talk to others about God's love for us, and the opportunity to accept Jesus into our lives and hearts, as only through Him can we be saved forever. We must share this message with others."

Jak pointed to the big screen where printed scriptures were shown, and he continued.

"Matthew 28:19 tells us:

'Go therefore and make disciples of all the nations, baptizing them in the name of the Father and of the Son and of the Holy Spirit.'

"In Mark 11:15-16 we are told:

'And He said to them, "Go into all the world and preach the gospel to every creature. He who believes and is baptized will be saved; but he who does not believe will be condemned."'

"Paul says in 1 Corinthians 9:16:

'Woe is me if I do not preach the Gospel.'

"And God's commandment is not limited to pastors and church leaders, but we are all tasked to spread the good news. There are people out there in our lives, your lives, yours, and yours, and yours who, right now, need some help, some guidance, someone to help them understand and accept Jesus, and get on and stay on the path. I know it's not easy. I'm trained to do this, and I still find it very difficult at times. We are often shy or hesitant to share our faith with others, and we can be met with resistance or people who simply do not want to be saved. In Luke 10:2-3, we are subtly warned:

'Then he said to them. "The harvest truly is great, but the laborers are few; therefore pray the Lord of the harvest to send out laborers into His harvest. Go your way; behold I send you as lambs among wolves."

"We, you and I, are the laborers." Jak pointed to his listeners. "And according to Psalm 119:46:

'I will speak of Your testimonies also before Kings, and will not be ashamed.'

"Finally, Jesus tells us: 'You are the light of the world.' *You* are the light, Jesus says." Jak pointed to us again, and then to himself. "I am the light, Stan is the light, my dad is the light, Eddy, and Jonathon, and Alisa are the light.

"Let's read that passage further. It's Matthew 5:14-16:

'You are the light of the world. A city that is set on a hill cannot be hidden. Nor do they light a lamp and put it under a basket, but on a lampstand, and it gives light to all who are in the house. Let your light shine before men, that they may see your good works and glorify your Father in Heaven.'

"Let's shine our lights on others. The light's intensity will change, sometimes bright like the sun, other times soft as a candle, not unlike a dimmer switch on some light switches. But may our light never be extinguished."

Jak paused and took a drink of water.

"Earlier, we witnessed the baptisms of Knowa, Keagan, Stan, Ashter, and Marcus. These are five people who have accepted Jesus Christ as their Savior, and I guarantee you that there was, or is, someone in each of their lives who has helped them decide to do so. Some of those helpers, laborers, beacons of light, are no doubt among us today. Who can you help? Whose life—whose soul—can you help save? Not just for now, but forever. It's an awesome opportunity, and responsibility."

Jak stopped pacing and stood at the pulpit looking as serious and determined as I've ever seen him. I had never seen this Jak before, as if he were not my son at all. I felt an inner tug of war between pride and shame. Why had I not seen this? My son was speaking so eloquently about God's Son. How could anyone want him to stop? His message switched directions a little.

"Several weeks ago when you hired me as your pastor, I know you were taking a leap of faith on an inexperienced, green leader. I promised you then that I would give it my all, and do my best. We live in very challenging times, and we are often pushed or led off the path by people or circumstances. As some of you know, we are being really challenged and tested increasingly lately. Well, today I want to reassure you brothers and sisters that I am even more committed today, and I promise to continue giving you one hundred percent of my leadership and commitment to spreading the good news about Jesus and accepting and keeping Him in your hearts and lives. I promise to help you stay on the path towards the Kingdom, and I promise to reach out to those of you, and others, who have not yet accepted Jesus as their Savior. And, consistent with today's message, I am asking you to help me, and to also spread God's Word and His promise for eternal salvation. Keep the faith, yes. But also spread it!"

What a wonderful message, with *these people* in attendance. Wait until Natas hears about this. But then, I'm not sure if that's good or bad. I subtly looked around and almost everyone had been fixated on Jak and his message. Some in his congregation really needed to hear this from Jak, fearing he would also give up. He continued and concluded.

"When Jesus returns on that glorious day, we need to each be ready and have him securely in our hearts and lives. But more than that, we need to be able to tell ourselves, and our Savior, that we did everything we could to bring others with us into God's Kingdom forever. Amen."

We all stood and sang "Joy of Our Faith."

After a time of sharing blessings and prayer requests, Jak concluded with prayer. After we sang one verse of "God is so Good", the service was over, and we were sent back out into the world, with or without Jesus in our hearts, which was up to us. I was never sorrier to see a sermon come to an end.

Would it be his last?

13

"**J**ak, you sit in front. I'll sit in back with Cherokee and Shelly." We got in, and Stan drove the Jag to Augusta for lunch and to go over the plan so far. "That was an awesome message, son." Stan and Cherokee quickly agreed. Shelly was staring astray.

"*These people*, and your people, really needed to hear what you said."

"Thanks."

"I bet Augusta is gorgeous—especially this time of year. The Masters is next weekend, isn't it?" I asked.

"Yes, it is, and yes it is," charmed Cherokee.

"Wow, are you a member?"

"No, I can't be."

"Oh yeah, is it still a men's only private golf club? I thought they might have changed that by now."

"Still men's only. We can live in houses on the course, and they'll take our money at the Club, the pro shop, and the pool, heck, if we're nice ladies, they'll even let us play golf. But if you don't have testicles, you can't be a member."

We all chuckled.

"Well, Cherokee, if you ever want to be a member vicariously, I offer my services as your pseudo member." I bit back the temptation to tender a testicle.

"Thanks, Rob, you know how many times I've heard that offer?"

"Well, the offer is still open."

"I'll file that somewhere. I did want to share something with you guys. I told Stan Saturday morning as soon as I found out, and thought I would try to help ease your minds over the weekend. Stan said he'd let me tell you today so you did not let your guard down, as you seemed to all be doing okay anyway. *These people* have decided, for now, *not* to kill anyone who they believe is saved. They want to save the opportunity to un-save them."

"I bet they're thinking that if they kill a saved person, since they have already been saved, they would go to the Kingdom, and therefore actually almost doing them a favor. Because it is not like once you are saved, you are always saved. You are vulnerable to be converted back to the bad side. So they decided that they are not going to destroy or kill anybody who is currently saved for now."

"That's exactly right, Jak. They are going to reserve the right to change that course of action, but as of now they are not going to kill or destroy anybody who is saved. They want to reserve the right to let Satan come into our lives and un-save us," Cherokee added.

"So Stan is still at risk with *these people*," I quipped, over-looking that he was just baptized. But that alone does not fix works in progress.

"Actually, we all are," Jak stated.

"Okay, but *these people* can change course anytime. Besides, how do they know who is saved and who isn't?" Stan asked and looked toward Jak.

"I don't believe they do. Just like we do not know about others, whether they are saved or not. They must just make assumptions based upon how people act," Jak responded.

"Well, let's hope they assume all of us are saved," I stated. It seemed like we all thought hard about how that assumption applied to us. There was silence for a while, so I broke it. "So, Cherokee, do you have a favorite golfer?"

"Yes."

"Can you share him with us?"

"Clue: He shared himself *way* too much a few years ago."

"Tiger?" I guessed.

"Yep," she tapped Jak's shoulder and added, "I tend to be drawn to the best."

"I understand."

"I hear you are pretty good, too, Rob."

"I try."

"Can I send you some contracts to review and negotiate for me?"

I paused. I saw an opportunity here. Lawyers can make good dough just doing legal work, but some get very rich by generating or originating clients or legal work for their firms. There are only so many hours in a day a lawyer can work and bill himself, so if he or she can manage clients with enough work for other lawyers to do and collect money for, that is where the real money is made. I looked at Cherokee.

She continued, "Hopefully, my criminal law needs are in the past, and Stan has my estate plan and philanthropy covered, but I'd like to move all of my endorsement contracts and business deals to McGill Hecker as well, and have you handle them, Rob."

"Well, I'm flattered, but I am also obviously pretty busy right now. However, if Stan would agree to give me all the origination on your new files, I'll gladly find the time and take them." I directed this more to Stan than Cherokee.

"Stan?" Cherokee also directed more than asked.

"How 'bout we split it, Rob," Stan suggested.

"Sure, and we'll split the credit on all your work and originations for Cherokee, too, Stan." I knew he had to agree, especially in front of Cherokee.

"Geez, Rob, save your negotiating skills for our clients' adversaries, not your partner. Anyway, deal."

If Cherokee's legal needs continued consistent with past practice, I probably just increased my annual income with the firm by one hundred grand or more. But I also probably just agreed to keep working my butt off.

"Great, guys. Rob, I'll have my assistant email you the draft documents, including some endorsement contracts for my new perfume line."

"Sounds, er, smells good to me," I cracked.

It did not take us long to get to Augusta National Golf Club. Stan turned into a long drive lined with shrubs, trees, and blooming flowers. The adjacent parking lot was packed with shiny Jaguars, BMWs, Mercedes, and late-model SUVs. We all just gazed at the splendor as Stan proceeded toward the club house for valet parking. Our car doors were opened by well-dressed teenage boys and Cherokee led us inside. Again, the door was opened by a charming young lad.

"Hello, Ms. Cherokee and guests, welcome to the famous Augusta National Golf Club."

"Thank you, Billy," said Cherokee as she gave him a generous tip to share with their team and motioned for us to follow her toward the dining area.

I doubted that Jak and Shelly realized it, but we were literally walking through a hall of history.

The hallway toward the restaurant was adorned with ornate glass-enclosed trophy cases and golf paraphernalia. There was lots of history about the exclusive club, a short member list, famous green jackets, old scorecards, videos of fantastic Sunday finishes, and tributes to the great ones, going way back to Hogan, Arnie, and Player. There was a great picture of Jack Nicklaus winning again in 1986, although past his prime. At that age, and mine, I appreciate what he did so much more. The photo of Phil Mickelson's first, putting on his green jacket, is one of my favorites. There's a Tiger den dedicated to Woods's great Masters championships, Cherokee's favorite. A man could spend all day reminiscing here, but we made our way to the dining room.

A middle-aged man in a tuxedo also welcomed Cherokee and announced, "We have your table for five ready over by the window." He grabbed five menus and led us to our viewing table.

The oak chairs matched the oak tables and were covered with silky white linens. Cherokee passed pleasantries with people at just about every table we passed en route to ours. As we sat, I noticed the sparkling china, sterling silverware, and crystal glassware. Not exactly fast food. Once I was settled in my chair, I virtually lost my breath. We were sitting next to a huge floor-to-ceiling picture window with the shades raised. What we saw outside was a collage of natural beauty and splendor, a picture only God Himself could paint. To me, and many, it was hypnotic. Just a few feet past the small outside-dining area was the practice green, where the golfers could practice their chipping and putting before their round. It was the smoothest green I had ever seen, one where it was difficult to define where the demarcation lines between rough, green, fringe, and chipping areas were. Did it break left or right?

Of course, the shrubs were vibrant green, and the flowers were blooming brightly. For the first time ever, I saw the famous magnolias and azaleas in person. I did not think it was possible that this place could be even more magnificent than it was made to be on TV. Some of the pro golfers had already arrived for next week's Masters Tournament and were practicing for their first practice round the following day.

They were practicing for their practice. That's why they're pros.

Even in practice, the pros walk the green slowly, steadily, as if not to break the thin ice below. They saunter from their ball over past the hole to check out the slope, the grain, the speed if possible, but make sure they do not take a single step on that holy ground between their ball and that magical hole in the ground. Past the practice green was a big oak tree which Cherokee explained was planted at the time the Club House and the course were constructed over

150 years ago. Beyond the big oak was the driving range, again more flowers and beauty. There were more pro golfers practicing their trade. You can almost tell if a golfer is a pro by watching his swing, even a practice swing. Whether it is a driver or a three iron in his hand, his swing, if perfect, is the same swing he's made millions of times before. Many variables affect the golfer's result. Some are based on the surrounding environment, the distance to the hole, the lie, the grain and texture of the grass, and the wind. Others are based on his own ability, his strength, his swing, his choice of club, and his control of emotion and adrenaline of the moment. If a pro gauges these variables correctly, and makes the right choices, he can hit that little white sphere pretty close to the target, be it 310 yards straight down the fairway, or a tricky nine and a half foot left to right bender on the green.

I remembered an amazing statistic about pro golfers. The average professional golfer finishes an eighteen-hole round of golf in about four to four and a half hours. During that round the average pro golfer hits the ball seventy-two times. Whether it be a drive off the t-box, or a putt on the green, each stroke averages about one and a half seconds. So, during that four to four and a half hours, the average pro golfer actually swings a club for a total of less than two minutes. Amazing.

But then, when you think about it, during our average day of sixteen hours of sleeplessness, we do not actually swing our clubs very long or often either, do we.

I finally snapped out of it as the waiter was taking our orders. After we ordered, I asked Cherokee to take part in our plan with Natas when she reported back and propose his meeting with Jak on Wednesday. Of course, I did not share the entire plan or details, since they were still in progress, and I was still not sure about Cherokee, but I tried to coach her on how to make Natas think that some of my suggested proposals and ideas would become his. She had some good follow-up questions.

"But if Jak is proposing the meeting, what do I tell Natas the meeting is for?"

"Simply tell him Jak wants to discuss the topic of his calling and Natas wanting him to stop."

"Okay, and I assume Natas will expect Jak to be making a proposal."

"Natas will expect a proposal, and Jak will make one" I spoke softly and went over parts of the plan. No one else spoke for a few minutes.

The waiter was now returning quite frequently with beverages and food, so I quickly concluded Cherokee's need-to-know on the plan, and the topics of conversation turned to more lighter and social subjects. Lunch was fantastic.

We finished eating and started walking back through the hallways of Augusta to the entrance.

"Do you guys have time to stop by the house?" Cherokee asked.

I looked at my watch, it was now almost 3:00 p.m. and I sadly replied, "Well, thank you so much Cherokee, but Shelly and I have a flight back home to Omaha at 4:00 p.m."

"It's almost three now, how are you going to make your flight on time?"

"Well, we're flying privately, so if we leave now we will make it to the airport in plenty of time. We brought all of our stuff so Stan can just drop us off."

"Private, huh? The firm must be doing well these days," Cherokee directed to both Stan and me.

"It's a client's jet, and we worked out an arrangement for a few flights in exchange for a discounted fee arrangement," I explained.

"I see. Maybe we can discuss this arrangement sometime with my planes. I can't remember the last time I flew commercial."

"You have your own planes, too, Cherokee? I'm surprised Stan hasn't discussed some bartering with you."

"Well, right now I only have one. I like to keep at least two in case one is in use or in for maintenance. But about a month ago, I sold my Cessna Citation to Jeremiah Kamp. You guys probably know of him I'm sure."

We all nodded affirmatively.

"His band was looking for a good used jet and made me a good cash offer, one that I thought would probably exceed any trade-in value I could get. I liked that jet model, so I might just buy a new one."

"That's awesome. But we better be heading to the airport."

"Ok, I'm just going to hang around here and probably have a drink in the lounge. I'm sure I can get a ride to the house. I will be in touch after I contact Natas."

I went to give Cherokee a good-bye handshake, and she insisted on a hug. I learned firsthand why her fragrance lines sold so well.

Stan summoned the valet guy for our car, and drove us to the private terminal.

Flying by private jet is so much better than flying commercial. No need to arrive two hours ahead of time and park too far away. No long walks and lines to wait in. No trains, trams, people movers, or annoying scooters beeping by. No need for a boarding pass, and maybe best of all, no security check or risk of a strip down. No waiting at the gate to enter the loading chute when your turn is called to board the bird. No cramming in with a hundred or so other passengers trying to fit square bags into rectangular bins, some while holding a laptop and a child while fiddling with their iPhone. No, private aviation has none of these annoyances and inconveniences.

We entered the airport from the south side where they hangar the private jets. It was 3:45 p.m., right on time for our 4:00 p.m. departure. Stan parked us right in front of the small terminal and stayed in the car while Jak helped Shelly with her luggage. I offered to carry one since I had none.

"Are you sure you don't want me to stay here?" Shelly sadly asked Jak.

"No dear, you go home, be steadfast, and stay on the alert." Jak was firm.

"But my home is here now with you." She reached for him and hugged him hard.

Jak grabbed her shoulders and looked into her teary eyes. "I know, but I want you to go to Omaha with Dad and stay with your parents. It will be safer for you. Dad said he can arrange a flight back here for you when the time is right. A free flight." Jak tried to make light of the moment, but Shelly had none of it. Neither did I, and kept my distance in the parking lot.

"But I'm going to be worrying about you day and night." She hugged him again not wanting to let go.

"I'll be fine. We'll be fine dear. Your flight is in ten minutes. Now let Dad help you with your bags." He kissed her and whispered in her ear.

"I love you, too, Jakson Andru. Now promise me you'll be fine."

"I will be, no matter what." He disengaged their embrace and started to get in the car.

"Thanks, Dad. See you tomorrow night or Tuesday morning."

"Ok." I picked up one of Shelly's bags but she stood still, staring at the Jag's tail lights, not knowing when she would see him again.

"Come on Shelly, we'll be fine."

Her shoulders slumped as she bent over to get her suitcase and we proceeded slowly inside to check in. Milo's fleet chartered through Elliot Aviation, and Shelly and I were greeted at the desk by a nice woman.

"Hi there, my name is Ellie, how can I help you two?"

"We're here for a four o'clock to Omaha courtesy of Milo Schneider."

"Oh yes, you must be Mr. Robinson Ross."

I nodded and she looked and smiled at Shelly, whose still-wet eyes did not meet Ellie's.

"And this is Shelly Ross, my daughter-in-law. There will be two of us."

"Super. Your pilot is right there," Ellie said as she pointed out a large picture window at what I assumed was our ride home. It was a King Air C-90 six passenger jet. "He's topping off the fuel and re-stocking the snacks. Oh, here he comes." The man headed towards us.

Ellie handed over the flight manifest to the pilot. "Your two Omaha passengers are here. Mr. Ross and his daughter-in-law, Shelly."

"Hello there, and thank you for flying with us." He put out his hand for a shake and gestured to take Shelly's bags. I only had my briefcase. "My name is Pontius, and I'll be your pilot, flight attendant, and first responder in case of need for a rescue." He grinned and motioned us to follow. "Oh, and don't blame my parents, it's just a nickname. If it matters, my real name is Peter."

We walked about fifty feet on the tarmac, and took about three steps up some hanging stairs and climbed in. Pontius boarded last, drew up the stairs, and locked the door.

"Make yourselves comfortable and fasten your seat belts. I'll fire her up and take off."

The familiar buzz of the engines would make chit-chat difficult but Shelly was already plugged into her iPod anyway. I had never really connected with her, though Sheryl and I were getting closer to our new daughter-in-law, and I really liked her before she and Jak moved to Atlanta. She looked tired and understandably stressed. Her attitude toward family, and life, seemed to have changed over the last few months. Even over the last couple of days I sensed a difference about her. Maybe there was another reason Jak thought she should go back to Omaha for a while.

We only taxied for about thirty seconds and took off smoothly. I opened my briefcase to work on some draft contracts that needed revisions to tilt them back in the favor of our clients. In my briefcase was another plus of flying private—being able to transport a Colt .45 and ammo. I gazed out the window as we ascended ever so gently. I glanced at my watch, not so much to be able to bill a client, as to marvel in the joys of flying private. It was 4:02 p.m. This is the only way to fly. Lucky Milo.

An email came in from Cherokee's assistant with several contracts attached for me to work on. Also included was an executive summary of each deal, some background, and some of Cherokee's thoughts and objectives.

Separately, Cherokee sent this email to me, Jak, and Stan:

Natas has agreed to meet Jak at Turner Park, but moved it up a day—Tuesday at 2:00 p.m. Just he and Jak. No weapons. He says he will recognize Jak. Can I confirm we're on?

Jak already replied: *Yes, thanks Cherokee.*

I did some more work on the flight as Shelly slept, listened to who knows what on her iPod. Pontius yelled back and told us there were snacks and drinks and pointed to some drawers and a medium-sized fridge. I got up and looked inside. Soda, water, beer. Decisions, decisions. The King Air purred along smoothly at 515 mph, twenty-four thousand feet above probably Tennessee, or even Missouri by now. Too high to see Kraig's future XXX assets below. An LED monitor gave passengers the speed and elevation details. It took me the whole flight to get through Cherokee's documents and make notes. I would finish in the morning and send her my thoughts and recommendations. It looked like she had a little leverage. We were descending, so I downed my drink.

We landed in Omaha and taxied another thirty seconds to the terminal. I asked Pontius if he could check with Milo and fly me back to Atlanta tomorrow afternoon, since Natas moved the meeting to Tuesday. He said his schedule was open tomorrow after 3:00 p.m., but he would need to confirm with Milo.

We had touched down about 5:15 p.m. local time, and we were in the car about 5:30 p.m. I wished I owned a plane. Don't we wish we had a lot of things? I'm glad I don't have some things I don't want, but I also wish I did not have some things I do.

I dropped Shelly off at her parents' house and told her everything would be fine and to keep praying. She would not be returning to Atlanta with me. Jak had insisted. In fact, she never would make it back to Atlanta.

†

I went home to a most incredible, enjoyable welcoming party. I didn't even get through the doorway and Teddy and Bitty were going crazy—barking, yelping, squealing, jumping at my feet with their legs and tails wagging uncontrollably, begging for my attention and hugs. They do a mini version of this daily when I come home from work, but after being gone for three days, they were so happy to see me. It was hard for the feeling not to be mutual. What a pick-me-up after the last few days.

The welcome home from Sheryl was much more subdued.

"I cannot greet you with the enthusiasm of your little friends, given the circumstances."

"You never do, dear, but I understand."

"Tell me everything, Rob."

Sheryl had been getting updates via text and email, but I had purposely not talked to her too much because I wanted to give her my version and assessment of the past few days in person. In today's world of social media and selective memory behind the façade of anonymity and false pretenses, I wanted to give her all the facts without all the second-hand spin or forgetfulness, and let her know how I saw things unfold, the past few days and what our plan was for the next few.

So I did.

We sat in the kitchen as I talked, and she listened.

"Wow," she looked at me and said, "There is part of me that can't believe this is happening, but there's also a small part of me that can." I grabbed her hand a squeezed it. Mrs. Calm. I always loved that she was able to be a rock in these trials and appreciated it even more now.

"Have you heard Jak give a sermon since he became a Pastor?" I asked her.

"Of course not. We have not been to visit since he took the reins at the church."

"Oh yeah, I should have known. But you've heard him speak at Youth Group and as an intern."

"Of course. But how was it today?"

"I wish you could have been there. I knew he was pretty good, but his message this morning was nothing short of amazing. He surprised me today. He's got it, and for his followers that's great. But to *these people*, that's a bad thing."

I could hear Jakob coming up the stairs. He was already home from Creighton on Spring Break, as we live only about twenty minutes from its campus.

"Hey, Jakob," I said loudly before we could see him hit the landing and enter the kitchen. We hugged.

"You still know who's coming up and down, don't you? But what's going on? People on the web are practically predicting the end of the world again, but I've seen no reference to Jak or Natas, yet."

"The End might not be so bad right now, anyway. Sit down, son. I'll give you the *Reader's Digest* version."

I did.

I talked, and he listened.

"Wow, is there anything I can do?" Jakob asked.

"Yes, there is. Help keep a close eye on Mom and J'Nay here, and can you pick up J-Rod at the airport Tuesday around noon? He's coming home from Philly."

"Oh, sure."

"Also, Dad, yesterday when you called, my Caller ID said it was untraceable, or something like that."

I could not tell him the whole truth, so I did my best white-lying and told him that I got a new super-duper secure phone issued by the law firm. I explained that the firm knew all of us lawyers were talking on our cell phones with clients, and that given today's technology, our conversations were vulnerable to being joined or overheard by unintended or adverse parties. Not to mention our government. Although he knew, I again explained how the attorney/client privilege worked, and how the firm decided that they needed to issue secure phones to all the lawyers so that their calls with clients were secure. Otherwise, we would risk losing or waiving the attorney/client privilege, and our conversations would be subject to discovery by third parties and adversaries.

"It makes sense," Jakob said.

He was right. It actually did make sense. The firm probably should do this.

We all talked some more, and I was soon back downstairs in the man cave with Teddy and Bitty. We enjoyed some more TV, snacks, and relaxed a bit before bedtime. There was, at least, some temporary calm again.

14

The Sin Council meeting did not start until Natas entered and dimmed the lights at 8:31 a.m. The Dungeon was unusually cool, but the dark corner he occupied was cold.

"You're up, Lived. I want an update on Jak Ross. I personally called him and told him to stop, or else."

"Well, sir, he does not listen very well. I can also give you an update on Christian's attempts to seduce Victoria Wander, along with Ross's update. Remember how I told you last week that Victoria had a counseling session with that damn pastor and then attended his church last Sunday? Well, she cancelled her date with Christian, and all this past week she has been cold to him, resisting all his subtle flirts and lunch invites. She's been all-business and has requested that he be transferred from the soda beverages division to the mineral water section in a totally different building on the Coke campus."

"Damn it, that kid is a menace." Natas's blood was boiling. He stomped out of the room, ordered them to email him their reports, and cancelled the meeting. He was obviously going to have to deal with Jak Ross himself.

†

Monday, March 24

It was a calm Monday morning.

The day after Palm Sunday, and the start of one of the darkest weeks of Jesus's life. If our plan worked by Good Friday all this madness would be over.

I was up early and kissed Sheryl good bye. She, Jakob and J'Nay were getting ready to leave and go to the zoo this morning at my request for them to be somewhere public. There were only two morning arrivals at Omaha's Eppley Airfield with Atlanta departures, 7:35 a.m., and 9:45 a.m. I planned to tail *these people* and see what they were up to before I flew back to Atlanta in the afternoon. We had caught a break, but it was really *these peoples'* mistake.

Sometimes it's not so much what we do right, but what our adversaries do wrong. Thank you, God.

It seemed that Natas had sent an email intended to be for internal eyes only, identifying who they were sending to Omaha, but unintentionally copied Cherokee. Someone got burned again by technology by hitting the 'ol "reply to all" button. The careless email blast boomeranged back to bite 'em in the butt. Although they did not detail their plans or intentions, Cherokee knew who they were sending, and gave me a complete description. But we did not know which flight they were on, so I was at the terminal at 7:30 a.m.

I parked near the airport exit so I could tail their cab, or more likely their rental. I walked near the taxi and rental car desks and sat and waited. The nearby baggage claim LCD indicated the first Atlanta flight had landed, and people were starting to gather. About thirty minutes passed, and I realized that *these people* were not on the first flight, so I waited for the second flight and did some work.

Kraig Nelson was calling.

"Hi, Rob. The XXX deal is moving quickly. Richards is willing to give us the warranty and covenant not to further encumber his real estate, but he is being difficult on some other issues relating to inventory and the lease terms going forward. I don't know if he's playing hard to get or what."

"How's your business doing anyway? For that matter, how's the industry doing lately?"

"Actually, my businesses have done relatively well, but the industry has been depressed. We have held our own with our competition, and others in the industry, but it seems like the religious and social right-wing conservatives have not hurt business if you operate it correctly. Although, that might be why I'm able to buy Richards's stores at a fairly discounted price, because he has taken his hands off of the wheel."

The moral decline in our country and the fact that many people are moving away from the ministry should be good for Kraig's business.

"Kraig, if you don't buy Richards's stores, is there anyone else out there that might? I mean, do you have any competitive bidders against you? Anyone else also courting Richards's assets?"

"No, I am really the only one with cash since my stores and other businesses have done well."

"Well, then let's bluff a little bit. Tell Richards we'll forego the post-closing protections other than the covenant not to further encumber his properties. But on the real estate he is leasing to you post-closing, we want the previously agreed upon rents to be twenty percent less for the first two years, and then it goes back to what we agreed to previously. Also, on the leases, instead of ten-year terms, you'll only agree to three years with renewal options. Tell him you are worried about the declining, limping industry trends, and if you don't get this concession, you'll walk. You'll have more leverage in three years. No downside if there are no other buyers."

"Great advice. The lower rents will make the deal that much more attractive."

"You also mentioned an inventory issue."

"Yeah, two actually. First, he is getting out of the business, so he wants me to buy *all* of his adult toys and stuff. I'll take 'em off his hands but I don't want to pay Richards for little-used videos and toys nobody is watching or playing with, generating little or no revenue. I also only want to pay book value, and only for the good stuff. He wants replacement value."

"Agreed. What's the second inventory issue?"

"I am going to hire his general manager as my own GM for these stores. He's good, and he told me that he has a warehouse of popular videos and toys that he keeps at the ready to deliver among the stores as demand peaks. He refers to them as "off-balance sheet assets", partly to save taxes. They are videos and stuff warehoused or in circulation among the busier stores. But here's the deal, the GM says Richards has no idea these slippery videos and toys exist."

"Okay, go on."

"Well, I'm inclined to take those secret assets for free as an additional upside."

"How much is at stake?"

"The GM estimates over fifty thousand."

"Here's what I'd do. Lay out the new lower rents and shorter lease terms you are demanding, and then explain why. Tell him you are paying book value for only the good inventory, and nothing for the obsolete and slow-moving stuff that no one is watching or playing with. But, also tell him you understand that he has about fifty thousand of good inventory he does not even know about, but you fully intend to pay him for it. You gain more credibility. This will help convince him to accept your other deal points. Besides, it's the right thing to do."

"I like all this, Rob. I'll reach out to Richards and be in touch."

"And, Kraig, be firm. You have the leverage position. At this point in the courtship, he's not going to get out of bed and walk, and my guess is he won't let you either."

"Thanks as always." *Click.*

I finished up with Kraig and also answered som questions via email with Milo and Cherokee on the respective deals.

After having reviewed Cherokee's draft contracts, an revising them in her favor from a legal perspective, I wantei to discuss with her the non-legal issues. The deal points the economics. I learned early on not to simply focus on a client's legal issues, but understand their business and no to wait for clients to call. Be proactive. So I dialed her.

"Hi there, Rob. You were on my list to call today."

Stan had explained how Caller ID still worked among our super secure phones. It was kind of neat to not only have a celebrity take your call personally, but also have you on Caller ID. And, she was going to call me.

"Hi, Cherokee. I was wondering if you had time to discuss your endorsement contracts in general and the Mon Vaur exclusive distribution agreement in particular."

"Uh, sure. That's kinda what I was going to call you about. I appreciate you calling me instead."

"Super. Let's discuss the Mon Vaur contract first, and then I think some of the concepts will apply generally to the other agreements and deals. Our diligence shows you've been with Mon Vaur for a few years, and this is a five-year renewal and includes some new brands, correct?" Eileen had actually pointed these points out to me.

"Yes, it's been a good relationship, but I did bid out the exclusive distribution rights for two of my cosmetics and one perfume. They were the second best bid, but I want to go with them because I like them, and it's easier if we keep them all together."

"I have made all the legal edits I think we need, but hav all the deal points been ironed out and agreed to yet?"

"No."

"Good. Does Mon Vaur know there is a better bid c the table?

"Yes."

"Okay. Good. Got it. You have some leverage. I see the consideration up front is only two million dollars, and then one percent per year on sales for five years. Is the two million market rate?"

There was a pause. "But I guess you bid it out, right?" I added.

"Yes, and again they were not the best bid, and their CFO tells me they have a cash flow problem right now." That was too much information from their CFO.

"Cherokee, what do your pro formas show for Mon Vaur's next five years of sales of your products under this exclusive deal?"

"About forty to fifty million per year, or $200-250 million total for the contract."

That was about what I figured based on my and Eileen's diligence.

"Okay, how about we propose that you help them and their CFO with their cash flow problem by a million bucks, and instead of two million up front, you'll agree to only take one million. But, in return you get three percent of the sales for your royalties. Do the math, Cherokee. You'll be *way* ahead."

"Great ideas, Rob. Can you revise the documents and send them to me?"

"Sure, and I'll send a transmittal email intended for you to easily forward to Mon Vaur. I'll include some cautionary words seemingly aimed at you that will cause Mon Vaur and their counsel to believe it's a good deal for *them*."

"Awesome. And one other thing. They want me to continue to make appearances at their stores throughout the country two to three times a month."

"Yeah, I saw that, but it only requires your best efforts. It is not a breach of the contract if you don't make the appearances. But the appearances could help you see a bump in sales of your products and therefore, your royalties. Have you noticed if the appearances increase your sales?"

"A little, but not much. The appearances are time-consuming and require a lot of travel. The juice isn't worth the squeeze for me. I think they want me to appear to increase overall traffic at their stores to help increase sales in their other departments. My sales and royalties are not increased that much."

"Ok, got it, let me guess. You do not want to do all the appearances?"

"No. I might once in a while, but nothing close to two to three times a month."

"Then I think you should tell them that, Cherokee."

"Um, I'll think about it."

"Tell them, Cherokee."

"Thanks, Rob, talk to you later."

†

The 9:45 a.m. Atlanta passengers were arriving. The two *these people* sent were actually pretty easy to spot. Stan speculated that, based on Cherokee's description, one of them was Chubby, one of the goons he ran into at Mrs. See's C-Store. Sure enough, there was Chubby—black t-shirt and brown jeans. Probably the same ones. But not No-Eyes. The other guy was about six foot four, on the slim side, and clearly the leader of the duo—firm build with silver hair and tinny-hued skin. Cherokee described him perfectly and referred to him as Tin Man. He had a limp and his joints even squeaked when he walked.

Now if Chubby pulls out an oil can...

They only had small carry-ons and by-passed baggage claims, and stopped at the Omaha Steaks Kiosk. I found that odd at first, but Tin Man bought a small set of cutlery knives. Crap. Then they went to the Avis counter, and Tin Man paid cash, and got some keys. I headed on over to my car and drove over by the exit of the Avis lot to wait for them.

They got into a silver Chrysler, and as they pulled out I slowly followed out the exit. Tin Man was driving. Great, I thought. They send the one with no heart. Why not the Scarecrow, or even the Lion? This guy probably has brains, courage, and no heart. Dang.

I felt weird, scared actually, tailing *these people,* wearing a loaded ankle holster. Tailing someone did not end up too well for my tail, Gil Egan.

They headed northwest on Abbot Drive, the first sign that their intentions matched my hunch. I had guessed they would go to our place, and they were on their way there. Good thing no one was home but the dogs. I'd protect them too if I had to. They drove the direct route we take from the airport to our house. It only took about fifteen minutes, and we approached our street, but *these people* went past our house and drove about one more block. They slowed as they passed our house, but they proceeded to the church. I watched them park, but I went around the block to the back of the church. I serve on our Board as Treasurer, and have a church key, so I knew I could enter from behind.

Pastor Mac Korver's car was parked in the front lot, and I figured *these people* were going to pay him a visit. Darn it. They knew Pastor Korver and Jak were close. I went in and downstairs to the church basement, and up some backstairs, the back way to Pastor's door from the basement.

I took the stairs very slowly and quietly and could hear them threatening Pastor Korver. It sounded like they wanted him to stop his ministry, too, and they said they might also harm Gayle, Pastor Korver's wife. But they also wanted Pastor Korver to convince Jak to quit. So I went back down out of earshot and called the police. When I returned to the top step, I could hear Tin Man speaking.

"Call Jak as we have demanded, or we'll cut a finger off to start." I was not sure if I was up to this. This was new territory for me. Did I have the intestinal fortitude, the guts? Sure, I did. I bent over and un-holstered my gun and cocked the hammer. No guts, no guns, no glory.

I steadied my Colt .45 Peacemaker and swiftly swung open the steel door.

"Stop it," I yelled and pointed the .45 at Tin Man. He had a steak knife at Pastor's finger but then put it at his neck. I looked around but did not see Chubby. He was behind the door, and pushed it at me very hard, knocking me down and the gun out of my hand. It shot a bullet into the bookshelf. Chubby was coming at me with another steak knife, but I kicked him in the groin, very hard, and he went down squealing like a pig. Tin Man made a move toward the gun but I tripped him and he ended up stabbing himself in the stomach. I reclaimed the .45, re-cocked quickly, and told them both to freeze.

Pastor Korver watched helplessly in disbelief.

I directed them to put the knives on the desk and get in the corner. I told them that if they moved I would put some lead in them. Tin Man's cut was minor. Two squad cars pulled in, and I opened the window and shouted, "In here, officers. I have a gun, holding two assailants at bay." Just as the officers came in, I put the gun down, showed two empty hands, and let them take over. They secured and took the weapons and began their questioning. Chubby and Tin Man were arrested and taken downtown to the police station. Pastor Korver and I were also ordered downtown for more statements, but were allowed to take my car, albeit with a police escort.

On the way downtown, I called the city attorney, Paul Katzer. I have his personal cell number because we are good friends, and go way back. We used to be partners at a prior law firm until he was appointed by the mayor. I helped him get the coveted appointment, and he's never forgotten. I also helped him with his separation from our firm. My partners initially offered him an embarrassingly low severance package. I mean, he was not going to another firm to compete with us. He was going to be the Omaha City Attorney—in a position to help our clients and refer us work. Sometimes, even long-time partners can be very short-sighted. I basically represented Paul against my firm. I convinced my partners to significantly sweeten his severance. I helped Paul and myself, I guess. The firm now gets a lot of the city's outside legal work when Paul or his staff need help.

Paul and I have also golfed together for years. You can tell a lot about a man by playing a round or two of golf with him. How does he handle adversity like an errant tee shot into the trees? How does he react to a bad break, like his ball landing behind a shrub, in a divot, or in a fairway bunker? Does he fudge, accurately keep track of his strokes and score, comply with the rules, and follow the game's etiquette? Does he take risks? Does he boast in victory, or handle a loss with dignity? How does he treat the guys in the pro shop, or the gals on the beer cart? Does he cuss? Throw a club or two in disgust? Can he give an appropriate compliment? Golf can bring out a person's emotions and character; the good, the bad, and a lot in between.

Well, I only needed to golf a couple of rounds with Paul to know that he was a man of character, honor, trust, dignity, and humility. I trust him with my wife and my wallet.

"Hi, Rob," he answered.

"Hey, Paul."

"Hi there, I suppose you're gonna be thirsty later." Paul stated the obvious. We often met after work for a beer.

"That could be, Paul, but I need your help."

"Well, I'll see what I can do."

I explained the situation to him, and he agreed to meet us at the station.

As we drove downtown, Pastor Korver explained to me that Tin Man and Chubby were threatening him with the knives unless he called Jak and counseled him to seriously consider ceasing his ministry, or else. Pastor was pretty shaken up.

After we gave our statements, Pastor Korver and I were allowed to leave, but met up with Paul and one of his best assistant city attorneys, who proceeded to talk to the policemen to discuss the appropriate charges and handling of the suspects. Pastor Korver went down the hall and made a phone call. I met with Paul.

"Rob, what's this all about?"

I gave him a condensed version of the past few days, leading up to Pastor's assault.

"Wow, Rob, so what do you want me to do?"

"I've never asked you to compromise your position, or pull any inappropriate strings, and I never will. But what kind of charges will be filed, and how long can you keep them in custody?"

"Well, we'll have to work with the County Attorney's office since a felony is involved, but we'll keep them overnight on charges of assault with a deadly weapon, terroristic threats, use of a weapon to commit a felony, and possibly more. Arraignment is tomorrow morning at nine, and whether we can keep them after that will depend on whether they can make bail. The bail amount depends on a lot of factors, such as the facts we can prove so far, their criminal records, risk of flight, and danger to others, as well as the testimony tomorrow morning by you and the pastor."

"We need that bail to be set as high as possible, and remember, I'm going back to Atlanta in about an hour, so I can't appear tomorrow and won't be here to monitor these guys if they make bail."

"Oh yeah, well, we'll have to go with the pastor's testimony then."

"Can you attend the hearing with the pastor?" A favor I *could* ask for.

"Sure, along with my top deputy."

"Okay, and Paul, they ticketed me for possessing a firearm without a permit, and confiscated my .45. Can you do anything about that?"

"Not too smart, Rob, but since you have no record, it's only a small fine."

"But can you help me get my gun back?"

"Sure, but not until you get the permit."

"Okay, that will have to wait. I need to get the pastor back to church and get to the airport. Thanks for everything, Paul."

"You bet, but you owe me a cold one."

"You got it. See you later."

I drove Pastor Korver to the church and prepped him for the arraignment and his testimony. I told him to try to get in as much as possible about the Dark Angels, and what led to the assault and the charges. "We need big bail to keep these jerks in jail."

"But isn't a lot of what I know considered hearsay?" he asked.

"Yes, but hearsay evidence is admissible at an arraignment and bail hearing," I explained. "Call me tomorrow afterwards, and Mac, good luck."

I dropped him off at the church and stopped home quickly.

The pastor's wife had called Sheryl, so she was already up-to-speed. "Did you really pull a gun on *these people*? When did you get a gun?" She deserved more but I was short of time and short with her.

"I'm sorry, yes. But it served its purpose, and I cannot give you a covenant not to repeat it." Pause. I was out of character. "Dear, I fear our lives have been changed forever. The boys will be home tomorrow. Meanwhile, keep the doors locked and dogs alert. Oh, can you pick me up some chocolates for Mom?"

"Sure. I visited her yesterday. She said you called."

"Thank you. I'll take her the chocolates when I return later this week."

I was late so I grabbed my bag, gave her a kiss, Ted and Bit a hug, and headed to the airport.

Milo had agreed to have Pontius fly me back to Atlanta around 3:30 p.m.

I was late, and we still had very little leverage. I was going to change that.

15

He had called a late day meeting of the Sin Council. They had been following closely the much-publicized trial of Hans Dirt, who was accused of murdering a rival mob boss with his bare hands. At first, forensics felt that the victim had been bludgeoned to death with a baseball bat, but later discovered data that determined that it was Dirt's fists that had done the swinging. He was the kind of big, bad boy who sins enough and needs no nudging from the Sin Council. But they were interested in hiring Dirt. He would have been of little use to them behind bars, but the verdict had just come in, and the jury acquitted him based on self-defense.

From his dark corner, Natas addressed the Council.

"By now, you know that Hans Dirt was acquitted and freed. Lived, you've led some of our past efforts to hire him and his mob to help carry out some of our more serious transgressions. He's denied our offers to scoop up his team. However, he's been locked up for several months fighting an expensive legal battle. His *businesses* have taken a hit, and some of his members have defected. Lived, I want you to dust off Dirt's file and see if he would now be interested in helping us on a contract basis. You don't need any more details, because if he has an interest I want to talk to him and negotiate the details myself. I can meet with him anywhere, anytime. I want you to contact him and congratulate him on his acquittal right after our meeting."

"Will do."

"While we're here, Sinbad, can you give us a quick update on the Free Drug Drive Initiative?"

"Yes, sir."

Sinbad proceeded to report on how his team was giving away free drugs to co-workers and friends, mostly marijuana and coke. Some refused, but they knew which recipients were likely to accept the giveaways. Many of them had already become drug-buying customers of the Dark Angels' drug trade. But the resulting revenue was really only an added benefit. The real objective of the initiative was drug addiction. Once addicted, the Sin Council could close their file on a person, as sin and bad choices came naturally without any of further nudging. Sinbad's boss and his boss's boss were pleased. Indeed, the devil was dancing in delight.

"Good work, Sinbad. Lived, let me know as soon as you make contact with Hans Dirt. He'd be a good replacement for Gil Egan."

†

I spent most of the flight back to Atlanta on the phone and answering email. Just me and Pontius on board. These private flights seemed to go so much smoother, and faster. I did not work on work. I was working on our leverage. Several cell calls and emails from thirty thousand feet proved fruitful.

Stan picked me up, and had another gun for me. We stopped and picked up a twelve-pack of beer and sandwiches, and arrived back at Jak's around 8:00 p.m. I had already debriefed them on what happened and reassured Jak that Shelly was safe with her parents. I first went inside to drop off my bag, put the now ten-pack in the fridge, and freshened up.

Jak and Stan were on the porch.

†

"Jak, Rob asked you about me, so it's only fair I ask you if you think he is saved," Stan asked.

"I think so, but Dad has made mistakes and fallen off the path at times, like all of us do. Nevertheless, his pastor, my pastor, Pastor Korver, in Omaha has helped him stay on course. And, I think I have helped him, too. But he, like all of us, needs to keep vigilant. And, can we go off the record, Stan, kinda like attorney-client privilege?"

"Of course, Jak."

"Stan, I think Dad is a work in progress, too."

"Really?" This gave Stan a good feeling to be in the same company as Jak's dad.

"Yeah, I have seen him struggle, partly due to his work details and dedication to daily demands and determination to deliver results. But don't get me wrong. If he died today, or Jesus returned today, I think Dad would join us in the Kingdom. But like us all, we are only truly saved if we have Jesus genuinely in our hearts either when we die, or on that glorious day when he returns. But the sooner we accept Christ and keep him firmly in our lives as our Savior, the better. Too many people figure they'll just wait until they get older and then live a life with the Lord at their side. But Stan, I guarantee you, some of these people will wait until the eleventh hour and Jesus will come again at 10:30. Besides, I believe people live happier and more blessed lives when they are believers, so again, the sooner the better."

"Hmm."

†

I returned to the porch. "Are you ready for tomorrow?"

"I think so, Dad."

"Okay, let's go over the plan again."

A pickup drove into Jak's driveway. Dan was joining us and would stay with Stan at the associate pastor's house. He already looked the part for tomorrow. Three-day stubble, a faded yellow tie-dyed t-shirt, holey jeans, worn Converse sneakers that had outrun their warranty, and disheveled hair.

"Perfect, Dan, you look ready for tomorrow," I told him.

"Oh yeah, let's do it."

We all settled in on the porch. I told them I wanted to make a call and then we would go over the plan again.

Jak called Shelly. No answer.

Dan and Stan both got on their phones and laptops, smoking Camels and enjoying Colt 45s.

I decided to dial J-Rod while we were all busy on the porch. I disarmed my Caller ID scramble.

"Hi, Dad."

"J-Rodder! How's it going?"

"Pretty good, just doin' some homework."

"Great, keep up the good work. Looking forward to coming home?"

"Yeah, but I wanted to get all my homework done so I have a calm, stress-free spring break." Good luck with that.

"Good idea. Maybe we can go golfing when you're back."

"That'd be good."

"Hey, Jak said you mentioned something about some people, anti-Christian types I guess, who try to stop people from being saved?"

"Oh yeah, there are some required theology credits here, and I am taking Theology 101. Last semester we started studying them. Very interesting, but kinda disturbing. For the most part they use fairly tame tactics and temptations to draw people away from Jesus, and try to convince people to live the good life. *Laugh with the sinners instead of cry with the saints* is one of their slogans. But they also use stronger tactics sometimes, including criminal activity, especially against Christian leaders trying to save souls. Dad, I know firsthand how good Jak is, that's why I mentioned *these people* to him. But why do you ask?"

"Oh, I think *these people* might be poking around his church or something." The understatement was intentional.

"Well, I'm not surprised. One of the things we learned is that the largest organized group is based in Atlanta—the Dark Angels. One of their MOs is that they often make their crimes look like accidents. Some of their lackeys have been caught and put in prison, but their leadership is very slippery and elusive." Once again, J-Rod knew more than I gave him credit for, but I did not want to tell him his brother was their main target as he had warned.

"Okay J-Rod, in your class, have you learned anything about how people can resist *these people* and their efforts— fight back, if you will?"

"Actually, Dad, we are just getting into that. One of our assignments over break is to read a chapter on that very subject. I plan on doing that tonight. But our professor gave us a preview, and it sounds like a lot of it involves prayer, of course, Bible study, and regular worship with others being part of a support system. Resisting temptations and always, always being vigilant and on guard, as we are all vulnerable. But Dad, I fear we may be fighting with one hand behind our back. *These people* will do things we won't."

"Agreed. I'm working on that. J-Rod, can you bring your textbook home? I want to read it, especially this chapter."

"Sure."

"Okay, thanks J-Rod. Have a safe trip home, and we'll see you tomorrow."

"Okay, love you." *Click.*

I guess others were listening in.

"Well, I sure as hell know how we need to fight back, Rob," Stan declared.

"Damn straight!" Dan echoed. "Stan got one already. I'm hungry to send another message to *these people*. And we don't need no textbook."

"Yes, you do, guys. It's called the Bible," I countered.

"Well, just remember, as Dan just referred to, that I saved your life by fighting back with my Colt .45."

"Well, I think I might be able to satisfy the appetite of you caged lions. I hired two guys today to help us, for leverage. You know one of them."

"Who?" Stan and Dan asked simultaneously.

"I've been busy on our plan. I hired Maxwell Dales Bazl today to help us."

"You've got to be kidding, I thought he was too busy, even after cracking the Sizak kidnapping," Stan said.

"Bazl on the case? Awesome," Dan added.

Maxwell Dales Bazl was one of the most prominent private investigators in the country. His adversaries feared him, for good reason. He often viewed the law as optional when he needed to resolve his clients' problems, but law enforcement usually overlooked it because he solved their crimes for them and gave them the credit. He just finished up rescuing the grandson of Reb and Don Sizak, successful real estate magnates in Omaha. The little boy had been kidnapped and held for seventeen days. The kidnappers demanded no police involvement, and the ransom was two million dollars. As usual, Bazl gave the police limited information, so they knew he was on the case, but could get no information from the Sizaks and were limited to what Bazl would share.

After resolving the kidnapping, rescuing the boy, and *accidentally* killing one of the perps, in self-defense of course, Bazl had given most of the credit to the government authorities. They loved it, and gladly took credit from the sidelines. They had no intentions of holding Bazl accountable for the perp killing. One less prosecution to pursue and process.

"What's Bazl gonna do for us?"

"Well, Dan, we need some leverage. Jak needs leverage. But I want to try to stay within the bounds of the law and the Bible as much as possible."

"C'mon Rob, we need a level playing field," Stan reasoned. "Stay with me here."

Jak had said nothing and was grin-less, but listening closely.

"I outlined a scenario for Bazl, and asked if he could help. He told me he had never done anything like it before, but it was doable, and although the timing is immediate, he and his team will be ready by tomorrow."

"What is it?"

"Bazl said although unique, it's actually one of the simpler assignments he's ever taken. There are a lot of moving parts, but it's all in process as we speak."

"Okay, okay, what is it?"

"According to Eileen's research Natas has a sixteen-year-old daughter, Sam. She attends Peachtree High School and ironically, is Student President of their Criminal Justice Department."

Dan and Stan were getting squeamish, but Jak was just listening patiently. At least someone trusted me.

"Well, I also happen to know the principal of Peachtree High, Gerry Batenhurst. Gerry and I graduated from undergrad the same year at Creighton, and often meet up at alumni functions. I took some education classes at Creighton, as did Gerry as he majored in education administration. I've been able to get people to move very quickly on this, and I convinced Gerry that he should have the great private investigator Bazl appear at Peachtree High. Bazl is scheduled to speak to the students at 10:00 a.m. tomorrow."

"How does that help? Jak meets Natas at 2:00 p.m.?" Stan looked at me as if I was crazy.

"I'm getting there. After his presentation, he is going to give Natas's daughter, Sam, an exclusive interview, since she happens to be the Criminal Justice Department's Student President. Bazl will wear a high-quality microphone during the interview and will record her voice saying some key words. Does anyone know where this is going yet?"

Silence, squinty eyes, and shaking heads by all three.

"Right after the interview, Bazl and his team are going to manipulate the tape. They will create an audio recording of Natas's daughter's voice and create a script of her on tape. If we need to tomorrow, we will call Natas's cell phone, and he will hear his daughter's voice, the voice of a terrified, crying sixteen-year-old girl, whom he will believe we have kidnapped."

"That's brilliant, Rob, but why don't we just actually kidnap the girl and let Natas know we really mean business?"

"That's out of the question, Dan." Anger and vengeance can motive people to say and do things they wouldn't do normally, although I really did not know Dan. But I was glad to be level-headed and that we were guided by a very competent minister.

"But he's gonna know it was a hoax, and it'll hurt our credibility next go 'round. Besides, what if he just calls his daughter tomorrow and calls our bluff?" Stan was sticking up for Dan and I could see that they were both tired of dealing with these Dark Angels.

"She won't be able to answer. Eileen looked up her schedule and the girl has classes from two to four tomorrow afternoon, and the kids cannot have their cell phones on in class. By the time Natas realizes he was duped, the meeting will be over, and hopefully, a deal reached."

"It's a very creative plan, Rob, and it might work tomorrow, but what about the next time, like Stan alluded to?" Dan asked.

"I think I have helped us in that regard as well. You see, to enhance our leverage with Natas, we need him to *believe* we will do some of the unlawful things you guys are suggesting. I think my other hire will help us with this."

"Well, I still think we need to do more," said Stan as he pulled out his .45. I ignored that.

"Eileen's research helped me find our second guy. I have hired an ex-associate of Natas', a bad dude who is best known on the street as a child molester and murderer. He goes by the name of Waster and needs some money. He was one of Natas's henchmen, but left the group on bad terms, and is quite willing to help us. Waster orchestrated and carried out some of Natas's more heinous deeds. When he got caught once, Natas basically threw him under the bus, and Waster served a few years behind bars. When he got out, Natas tried to make amends, but Waster basically told him to go to hell. Natas knows Waster is dangerous and will also take the law into his own hands on his client's behalf, so it's good to have Waster on our side, at least for this one assignment, and more if needed."

"What's he gonna do?" asked Stan with a perplexed look.

"Simple. All I really want him to do is make Natas think Waster has kidnapped his daughter and is on our side. He knows of Waster's willingness to walk the line, and his vengeful desire to get back at Natas. But all Waster has to do is call Natas tomorrow during his meeting with Jak, re-introduce himself to his old nemesis with much joy, and play the tape Bazl's team will get to him. Jak can reinforce to Natas that Waster is now on retainer with our side."

"I like it, Dad."

"Hmm," echoed Stan and Dan.

†

Stan, Dan, and I finished the Colt 45s out on the porch. They had some more questions, which I answered.

A pretty woman was walking by on the sidewalk. I saw Stan put his curled thumb and forefinger to his mouth to whistle at her.

"No, Stan! Good grief, you just got baptized yesterday. You need to act like it," I chastised.

"What? I'm single."

"How do you know she is?"

"Fine." He looked rather sheepishly at me, then Jak. They all went silent for a while, and got pre-occupied on those dang electronic gadgets.

I decided to call Kraig Nelson and make an investment. I allowed Caller ID to work.

"Hey, Rob. I have not gotten a hold of Richards yet."

"Good Kraig, because I am emailing you some more ideas to make your XX deal even more attractive. But I'm calling to tell you I'm in on the First Merit deal. I want at least two units."

"Did you review all that stuff already?"

Kraig and his partner, Tom Conardy, had a long successful track record of real estate investments, and I had helped them with their legal needs. I had formed another LLC for them to buy a commercial office building in Chicago, which the LLC would lease to the First Merit Bank. Kraig emailed me the Offering Memo the day before, financials on First Merit, the lease, and some SEC required docs. I was, again, doing the legal work, but also decided to invest in it. Lawyers invest in their clients, and their deals some times. Kraig and Tom had found another property that would return about eight percent based on the purchase price and rental income First Merit Bank would produce. But I had not reviewed all the diligence documents prior to committing a twenty thousand dollar investment.

"No. I didn't review any of that stuff. Kraig, I'm not investing in an LLC. I'm not investing in a strong tenant like First Merit; I'm not investing in real estate. I'm not investing in a lease. I'm investing in Kraig Nelson and Tom Conardy. I would not recommend a client do it this way, but my clients do not have my sense of judging people's talents, integrity, and ability to deliver. I see those in you and Tom. I'm not looking to invest or profit from a piece of paper or a piece of property. I'm investing in people—you and Tom."

"Wow."

"Take it as a compliment, Kraig, and prove me right again. I want at least two units. Talk to you later." There was more business opportunities I was willing to invest in that I wanted to discuss sometime in the near future, but we needed to get through this meeting with Natas first.

†

Jak had a call coming in.

"Hello?"

His expression took a quick turn toward troubling.

I could see Sheryl was calling me, but I did not take it.

"Oh my God, no. How badly?" Jak asked, clearly concerned. He paused and listened. "I don't believe it. That makes no sense. You guys baby your cars like children." He shook his head. "Okay. I'll start a prayer chain. Please keep me posted on Jay Jay and the investigation. Bye."

"Jak, what's wrong?"

"Unbelievable, Dad. That was John Anders. Jay Jay was in a bad accident this morning, and is in critical condition at Methodist Hospital. They had to take him by LifeFlight."

"What happened?"

"Apparently he ran a red light and was t-boned on the driver's side. A passenger friend, Julian, was also injured, but is in stable condition. Julian told police Jay Jay tried to stop but his brakes did not work. The initial investigation indicates that his brake fluid was empty. Dad, I suspect *these people* tampered with his brake fluid plug."

"No question about it, Jak."

I explained my visit from the neighbor a few nights before to Dan and Stan, warning of harm to Jay Jay.

"Dang, that can't be a coincidence, can it?" asked Stan.

"I doubt it. That's how *these people* operate."

"I'm going to the hospital, at least to be there for Jon and Alisa." Jak stood up and shook his head. He was all-business again knowing he needed to be strong for his parishioners.

"Okay, but try not to be late. You need a good night's rest."

"We'll see. But I'm ready for tomorrow. I like our plan so far."

Jak left for the hospital, and I went inside to grab three cold ones. I rejoined Stan and Dan on the porch and declined their joint offer of a smoke. I gave them each a fresh Colt 45.

"Those smokes will kill you guys."

"Funny. I've been hearing that for, oh, about thirty-five years now," Dan reasoned with sarcasm.

Stan took in a gratifying drag, and exhaled slowly.

"Rob, if *these people* did tamper with the kid's brakes, how the hell can we defend ourselves against such actions? And who knows what else they have done to cause further damage or harm to any of us down the line?"

"Oh, you can bet they have, and will Stan. Our lives have probably always been littered with land mines—some synthetic, some spiritual. But recently, due to *these people,* we can begin to connect the dots and picture heretofore accidents or coincidences as very damn real and contrived."

"Well, if we know who's doing these things, we need to fight back. And I mean really start fighting back. It's the only way to get them to stop."

"Stan, they will never stop. Besides, I suspect we do not even really know who *these people* are, or the extent of their reach and membership. They could walk right by us, or sit next to us on the bus or at the café. We just need to be vigilant and hope we have a higher, more protective presence on our side."

"Blind hope seems risky to me, Rob," Dan tossed in.

"Not blind. In fact, I'm starting to see how *these people* operate a little more clearly."

Stan, Dan, and I spent another hour or so on the porch, debating the various ways to combat whoever and whatever *these people* were, and their evil ways. They eventually wore down and turned in for the night next door. I was about to do the same when I saw some headlights pull in. But they meandered over to the church lot. It was Jak. He went inside. I waited several minutes, and then walked over to the church.

I entered through the front doors as he had, and made my way through the foyer to the back of the sanctuary. It was dark and quiet, but the moon shone through the stained glass and provided a brilliant soft hue. He was upfront in the first pew, staring at a single, still candle. As I slowly moved forward, my movement disturbed the peace. He calmly turned toward me and seemed to grin.

I saw so much of a child still in him. The little boy who liked to throw rocks and catch balls, the fast flag football player who I coached at the YMCA, and who made me look good as a coach because he would cross the goal line often, the kid who first loathed his guitar and piano lessons but learned to love them. The fledgling follower who found his future calling, our oldest child who had become a strong young man, the adopted son we had reared and raised best we could, who now led us if we would follow him. I sat next to him, but we said nothing for a few minutes.

Jak shook the silence, softly but so surely. "Jay Jay is in a coma." He took a deep breath. Though he was so strong I could see that this was taking a toll on him. "Dad, just so you know. I will never, never stop my calling." I put a hand on his broad shoulder that was already bearing so much and sighed.

"Let's get some sleep, Son."

16

Natas awoke early and sent his leadership team an email.

To: Sin Council
From: Natas
Subject: Meetings
Date: March 25, Tuesday – 5:59 a.m.

Sin Council:

This morning's SC meeting is cancelled. Just keep proceeding with your pending projects. Email me any significant updates, or any new matters you have opened since your last reports.

Lived, please send me updated stats on Ross. As you know, I am meeting with him today at 2:00 p.m. I don't know what I'm going to do with him yet, but I'm going alone.

Sinbad, if our guys in Omaha make bail this a.m. have them call me ASAP. I need them to keep their assignment.

†

Tuesday, March 25

I slept late and awoke about 8:00 a.m. and smelled coffee. Jak left a note that he had brewed a pot and was over at the church working already. I showered, did some work, and then called Stan to ask him and Dan to come over for coffee and toast on the porch.

Omaha City Attorney Paul Katzer called around 10:15. We needed bail set high on the thugs who threatened Pastor Korver.

"Hi Paul, how'd the arraignment go?"

"Not well, Rob. These guys hired, J. M. Davies, who, as usual, found whatever holes he could in the charges and evidence. And we drew Judge McGilly."

"Christ, Paul, aren't he and Davies golfing buddies?"

Paul did not need to explain to me that Davies is one of the best criminal defense attorneys in Omaha, and in the country for that matter. The Dark Angels probably had to pay him a pretty penny to take their case so fast. Big-boy cases come with big-boy price tags. Hiring Davies in a case before a judge he golfs with was a savvy move.

"Yes, and, of course, the worst part was that your pastor decided not to show up."

"*What?*"

"I assumed that you knew he decided not to press charges. He said he forgave them. We could still charge them based on his and your written statements, and their prints on the knives, but without live testimony the bail was severely depressed. Judge McGilly only set it at one hundred thousand each. They posted the ten percent and are free on bail."

"Crap. I gave Pastor Korver clear instructions on how critical the arraignment was, and how important it was to maximize the bail."

"I know, but I did ask the police chief to be sure to have his guys frequently cruise your church and house neighborhood."

"Great, thanks. I better call Sheryl and Pastor Korver."

"I already did."

"Thanks, I really don't want to talk to my pastor right now anyway. Keep me posted, and thanks, Paul."

"You now owe me two beers."

"Got it." *Click.*

†

Tin Man and Chubby were again on the loose in Omaha. They cabbed it to our church and regained their rental. They drove to Saul's Jewelry and Loan, a pawnshop not far from our house, and went inside. It was one of those typical shops to buy or pawn stuff. I loathe their ironic billboards. One shows a sparkling wedding band and says, *Need a loan? Give us a ring*. Pathetic, but effective.

The clerk asked how he could help them.

Tin Man explained, "We need a small handgun and a medium-to-large tree limb clipper."

For most people that would be an odd combo, but the clerk was un-phased.

"No problem, this table has a variety of handguns you can choose from, any one for forty-five dollars each, and I can throw in a good tree limb clipper," the clerk offered.

Tin Man chose a used Beretta semi-automatic, and the clerk included some ammo and an old scissors-like tree limb clipper. They flashed their permits, paid with cash and headed back to the airport.

†

Around 10:30, Jak walked back over from the church and joined us on the porch.

"How's Jay Jay? Any update?" I asked.

"Not good. He's still in a coma and critical condition. Sounds like if he makes it he may need a kidney transplant. A lot of internal injuries, in addition to his head trauma. And, to add insult to serious injury, the police have cited Jay Jay for running a red light and failure to yield."

"My goodness."

I did not explain to Jak, though Stan's eye caught mine indicating he understood, how the Anders were probably also at risk for civil liability due to perceived negligence. Failure to maintain their vehicle. The truth could be no further from fact.

"We'll look into it, Jak, and see what we can do. Have the Anders send me the citations and I'll handle them," Stan said. "And Rob, we can't leave this investigation solely to the authorities. We've seen how some of them work. Let's try to get the Anders family to hire us, pro bono. I want Jay Jay's wrecked vehicle sequestered, and I want to inspect it as Anders's counsel."

"Good idea, Stan."

"We should also try to back track wherever Jay Jay drove the car or parked it, and check for any brake fluid pools or leaks. If we can somehow tie *these people* to the lack of brake fluid, maybe we can dismiss the tickets, and pursue the perps."

"Thanks, Stan. But we still don't know if Jay Jay is going to make it."

"Do you know if he is saved?" I asked Jak. *These people* represented that they were not going to kill anyone who they believe was saved.

"Of course not, but I think he is."

"Do you think *these people* think he is saved? Why else would they try to kill him?"

"Dad, maybe they didn't."

†

It was after one o'clock, and Dan left to go downtown to Turner Park to find a place to perch by the park fountain. I told him not to actually beg for anything, just to look the part. He did.

Jak, Stan, and I remained on the porch for a few minutes and went over the plan one more time. I told Jak that it probably will not work out just the way we planned, so we had to be flexible and give Natas a little rope. Stan affixed Jak's mike to his undershirt and tested it. It was ready to go, and so was Jak.

I called Waster, and he told me that Bazl had just delivered him the tape. Bazl had told Waster the interview with Natas's daughter went well, and Waster said the tape sounded so real that he felt like he actually kidnapped the girl. He felt empty and cheated that the crime did not occur, but he was on standby and very eager to get back at his old nemesis.

Stan drove, and the ride to the park was quite quiet. It was sunny and a pleasant seventy-eight degrees. The radio was softly playing "Why Can't We Be Friends?" by War.

We parked a block from the park, and got out to go over the playbook. Jak was taking in the plan like a quarterback on the sideline during a timeout with his coaches holding clipboards. He left for the fountain to confront Natas about a minute before we headed to the boardwalk to watch and listen in. We were a few minutes early so he said he was going to walk the path the long way around the park to the fountain. As usual, he wore jeans, two t-shirts, and a determined, purposeful expression.

But I'll be damned, the kid was whistling when he walked away. Could have been grinning for all I know.

"Rob, you have one helluva son. Well done."

"Thanks, I am starting to realize that."

Stan and I made our way to the bridge overlooking the fountain. We soon realized that the man entering the park was clearly Natas. He looked weird, still at a distance. As Natas entered Turner Park, it seemed as if Satan reached up and increased his ability to do harm. Natas now had some nasty unnatural powers and a creepy, cruel way about him.

As he inched closer, neither Stan nor I said a word. What we were about to witness was unreal and unbelievable. Anyone or anything that caught Natas's eye or aura was in trouble.

As he walked along the sidewalk the green grass along its edges turned light brown, as if dead. The air was still, but bushes and branches bristled as Natas passed by them. We watched flowers wilt when he walked by. I gasped when a patch of healthy sunflowers slowly turned away from his glare.

He proceeded on the path and passed an elderly couple sitting on a swing enjoying an amiable afternoon. They pecked a kiss. Natas focused his eyes on them and stared intensely. Now the couple was arguing, the woman slapped her husband and left him.

Natas was getting closer to the fountain, the meeting place. A woman walking her dog was leaving the park going in the opposite direction. Natas studied the leash and caused it to slip from the woman's hand. She lost the leash and the dog when it darted out into the street and was hit by a car.

The figure reached the fountain and took a seat on a bench. Birds on the ground and on some overhead electrical lines all scattered and flew from him in fear.

Stan cringed and reached for his gun.

"Wait." I put a hand on his, and he re-holstered it.

We saw Jak enter the edge of the park's centerpiece. What we did not see was God's loving, graceful hand reaching down and lowering Natas's harm-ometer. Any superpowers he had been given were at least now temporarily gone.

The grass was green again. Stan and I saw the flowers regain their vibrant vigor and then we watched the sunflowers again turn towards the sun. The elderly woman was back and the couple held hands while leaving the park. The dog that was hit by the car was only slightly injured and now back in his owner's hands. The birds were back.

"Stan, did you just see all that?" I had obviously never seen anything like this before and was hoping I had company.

"I think so. How weird."

"Definitely not part of the plan." I was worried already.

Dan was instructed to wait and settle in at the fountain after Jak arrived. The park was not too busy as the lunch crowd was corralled back at their cubicles. There were only about five people around the large round fountain when Jak approached it, including a man on a bench throwing popcorn to the birds. Jak walked within four feet of the man, who spoke casually at first.

"Hello, Jak."

"Natas?" The man feeding the birds was Natas.

"Yes, good to see you again, Jak."

"Again?"

"We've not formally met, but I've been following you rather closely for a few weeks now."

"Great." He took his hand from his pockets and his eyes rolled as he spoke. He seemed completely confident and I wished I could feel the same way.

Natas was more visible now and appeared to be between forty and forty-five years old through binoculars. We were about two hundred feet away and elevated about twenty feet on a pedestrian bridge. He was about Jak's size, dressed in black slacks, a dark polo shirt, and a light black summer blazer. His thinning hair was a contrasting bleached blonde. His red shades shone like two little burning bushes.

Dan arrived and took a seat on the concrete circling the fountain, about twenty feet away. I told him not to be packing, but I couldn't trust him. He wanted *these people* dead.

There was another bench across from Natas, and Jak sat down. We watched with wonder as my son took a seat aside this insidiously evil figure.

"It is nice of you to feed the birds, Natas."

"How do you know it's not poisoned? Here, you want some?"

Jak did not answer. He noticed that Natas had not had nary a nibble of the popcorn as he looked, and seemed to briefly study, the birds and their condition.

"I seem to be at a disadvantage, Natas, as I suspect you know more about me than vice versa."

"You know, we actually have some things in common."

"I agree. We both seek, for example. I seek to save souls, while you seek to spread sin."

"Seems like you know more about me than I was lead to believe. Yes, we both try to influence people."

"But Natas, our objectives and means could not be more different. While I pray for people, you prey on people."

"I guess. Speaking of which, sorry to hear about Jay Jay."

"Spare me your insincere concern and sympathy, Natas. Besides, the investigation into that continues." Jak was getting mad and I saw him shift in his seat a bit. *Keep it together*, I prayed.

"Well, I do hope the boy makes it this time."

"Oh, he'll make it all right, no matter what."

Stan cringed when a dark cloud appeared over Jak and Natas, but they remained in bright sunshine. The smoky cloud did not create a shadow, and Jak had no idea it was above him.

"My gosh, do you see that?" I turned toward Stan and he was visibly shaking and freaking out. He could not answer.

"You know, if you would just do as we ask and stop your calling, things like your pastor's assault, Jay Jay's accident, and many other issues and problems in your followers' lives might not happen."

"So, why me, Natas? I've only been doing this for a few weeks, at least officially, and I am only twenty-two. Do you really think I can harm your cause?"

"You may be young and green, but my leader is very observant and prophetic, and he already sees you as a major threat. We've found that people who have accepted your supposed Savior through the guidance of leaders like yourself are very difficult for us to convert back to the un-saved. When we try to condemn people with our sin attractants, such as temptation and greed, they are easier targets if they have not been assisted by the likes of you."

"But hell, I've only been doing this for literally a few weeks," Jak countered. He was frustrated by Natas's comments.

"Oh, even you swear, huh, Jak?"

"Not really, it's certainly not using my Lord's name in vain, and I'm probably just referring to your future homestead."

"Whatever. But again, my leader sees your potential. In fact, you probably don't even know this, but your statistics are off the chart."

"My what?"

"By our measure, your Sunday attendance has grown every single week since you started, and you have already averaged, between your Sunday and Wednesday services, over four baptisms per week. Your attendance is up seven percent and the Youth Group is exploding. Your run rate is scary as your following grows. These are impressive by themselves, but what really scares us is that your retention rate is ridiculous."

"What?"

"You probably don't keep and review the data that we do, but our massive research, led by our IT department, shows that in most churches an incredibly large majority of people who are saved during the typical Sunday baptism, can be un-saved by us by Monday or Tuesday with more sin attractants. But so far, between your two weekly services, from what our intelligence shows, your thirty-five baptisms to date have stuck incredibly well. To your credit, despite our efforts, we have been unable to un-save all but one of the people you have supposedly saved. Of course, we'll stay after these people, but the statistics you have already garnered actually kind of scare the hell out of us." While Natas was speaking a foggy gray hand began to descend down from the cloud headed for him.

"Well, I guess that's the best report card I've ever received." Jak grinned. Natas scowled. The hand stopped short of Natas and receded up inside the cloud.

"So that should explain to you why we intend to stop you, and that is why we are here today. But just to make sure you know we mean business, and that if you do not cooperate we will take some painful actions, I want you to take the phone call that is about to come on your cell phone right about ... now, and put it on speaker."

"Hello?" Jak answered, very tepidly.

17

I could hear a familiar voice through Jak's mike. "Jak, I'm sorry. *These people* have me and Jakob and are threatening some bad stuff."

Oh my God. I tensed, ready to run toward Natas with murder in my heart. It was J-Rod. Stan put his hand on my shoulder to steady me. Now I was shaking. We could see Jak sit up and try to strengthen his posture and his will.

Stan and I watched as another arm extended down from the gray haze toward Natas, but quickly retreated as if slapped away.

"As you can hear, we intercepted your little basketball-playing brother and have him and your other brother in custody as insurance in case we can't come to an agreement here today. We only intended to capture J-Rod, but Jakob fell into our hands when he was picking up his brother at the airport. Your dad tried to keep my guys locked up in the Omaha jail, but we posted bail, and now they have your siblings. So we have some double indemnity insurance. At the very least, if you don't cooperate we intend to clip the right index finger right off J-Rod's shooting hand."

Jak looked at his phone and asked, "J-Rod, are you still on?"

"Yeah." One word was enough to evidence J-Rod's voice was crackling and trembling.

Jesus Christ, what on Earth had we gotten ourselves into? I tried to come up with something to turn the tides back to our favor, but I could simply pray. "J-Rod, you know no matter what happens you are going to be fine, right?"

"Yes, Jak. Do what you need to do." Somehow, J-Rod suddenly sounded composed. Jak's words calmed him, and also me. We'd have to trust in our plan, and God's plan.

"Enough. Shut off your phone, Jak."

"Fine, Natas. But I will tell you this, if you so much as clip J-Rod's fingernail, or harm Jakob, I will come after you with every Earthly and heavenly power I can muster and make sure I...."

"Make sure you what?" Natas challenged him.

"I don't know. Maybe I just simply not try to save your soul so you end up in the homestead I referred to earlier. That would be much more everlasting retribution than anything I could do to you now."

Homeless Dan stood up and thought about moving in to force a timeout, but was beat to the punch by a real homeless man. A very thin, unshaven, unkempt man approached Natas, and asked him a universal question.

"Can you help me, brother? I am out of work and hungry."

"Get lost, loser." Natas quickly dismissed him with intended narcissism. He did not even offer him some popcorn, so maybe it was not poisoned after all.

Real Homeless dropped his shoulders and turned his empty stomach and head toward Jak.

"How about you, brother?"

Jak had already gotten out his thin wallet, though there was not a whole lot in it for himself, and looked the guy in the eye. "Here's a five dollar bill, brother, and please pray for yourself and others," he said warmly.

Real Homeless was clearly grateful and mumbled "God bless you" to Jak and was on his way.

"Touching. Now back to our situation," Natas demanded. "You probably do not know this, but we sent two of our people to your service this past Sunday. Some message you delivered Jak. More proof of your troublesome potential. Our guys duly filed their report on what they saw and heard and promptly resigned from our organization. We suspect they may join yours."

"Good," Jak grinned.

"Bullshit. We've had enough of your crap, enough of your dad's crap, and enough of Stan's crap." Natas's voice was up a few volumes now. "You stop saving people, or your brother will need to develop a left-handed shot!"

I was tired of Natas's threats. We needed to take control over this situation again. I had Waster on the line and he was ready to call with the tape from Bazl. Jak was aligned.

"Well Natas, I think it's your turn to take a call. You're about to hear from an old friend, or should I say ex-friend."

I gave Waster the green light to call Natas.

"We've recently hired one of your ex-handlers. I understand he served some time for furthering your cause, but seems he's wanted to even the score ever since you double-crossed him."

Natas's phone was beeping a god-awful ring tone.

"Why don't you put it on speaker, too," Jak suggested.

"Natas here."

"Well, well, well, Natas, our paths cross once again. It's Waster."

"Hey Waster, you sure you don't want to rejoin us?"

"To the contrary Natas, I've taken an assignment with the other side. Besides, I owe you."

"I'm in a meeting, Waster."

"I guess you could say so am I, ha ha ha." Waster sounded like he was enjoying this.

"Waster, what do you have for me?"

"Oh, it's not what, Natas, but who? I have someone here who is just dying to talk to you."

"Daddy, it's Sam."

She sounded terrified, her voice manipulated to resemble a crying girl. A kidnapped crying girl.

Natas stiffened, looked at his phone, and looked like he touched a livewire. Then his eyes pierced Jak like Satan's spear.

Jak didn't blink.

"Daddy, this man grabbed me and pushed me into the back of this van. Someone drove us away, but I do not know where we are. He keeps touching me, Dad. I'm scared. Get me outta here, please!"

"Are you okay? Have they harmed you, Sam?"

"Not yet, Dad, but this guy's a creep." Bazl's team had done quite a job with the tape.

"Careful, little bitch, or I'll creep closer to your cuteness." Waster was on speaker and threatened his make-believe victim.

"Waster, it's Jak," Jak shouted at Natas's phone. "Don't harm the girl. Just hold her for now, and don't touch her or do anything until you hear from me or Rob."

"Oh, all right. You're the boss. Later." Waster hung up. Jak was oblivious to the cloud above and its attempts to reach out and touch Natas. It tried again but the arm did not drop very far before elevating back up. But I thought I saw some lightning within the billowy haze. Was there also a battle going on in there?

Natas was boiling, but simmered down to try to work this out. He was studying Jak intently. This had become a very high stakes poker game. Natas held some strong cards and a solid hand, but he thought Jak had one, too.

"Okay Jak. I sense your damn dad did this. I'll order the release of your brothers if you tell Waster to free Sam."

"Sounds reasonable, but let's first come to some type of agreement going forward. And remember, we have Waster on retainer, and if he has to free the girl I'm sure he will not consider the score evened with you."

Natas's horns had seemed to recede slightly.

"Jak, you have proven to be a freaking formidable foe from the start. What do you have in mind?"

Jak decided to try a bluff. He floated the net-net concept he and I had discussed. "Natas, if I agreed to stop, would you?"

Natas countered, "If I did, would you?"

"If you truly agreed to stop spreading sin and un-saving and harming people, I *might* agree to stop saving souls."

"I'll have to think about that one. But I doubt either of us could just stop."

"You know I am not going to agree to give up my calling and willingly stop saving people. And I know you are probably not going to stop destroying people and un-saving them. But good and evil have co-existed since the beginning of time, and there must be a solution here."

"I have a proposal, but first let me ask you this. Do you really think you can change my heart, Jak?"

"No, but God offers you a new one—a transplant. Listen to him through Ezekiel 36:26:

'And, I will give you a new heart, and a new spirit I shall put inside you, and I will take away your heart of stone and give you a new heart.'"

"But Jak, a heart transplant requires that someone else has to die, no?" Natas thought he had Jak on a technicality.

"That's right. God's Son has already died for you and us, and offers his heart to us if we just accept him."

"Okay then. In my infinite wisdom I have come up with a brilliant plan, a proposal that if you agree, can bring an end to this madness, at least for you and yours, at least for now."

"Let's hear it."

"Okay, Jak. And if we can't come to terms, and you don't quit your calling, we will have to inflict harm on you, or some of the souls you have saved. Maybe even introduce some of them to your so-called spiritual la-la-land a little early."

"Well, you'll be too late, as they are already saved and will have defeated you. If they could, they'd probably send you a thank you card. If you kill a saved person, you lose."

"Clever, Jak, but good point. Instead we could go after the ones you have not quite saved yet. Your *works in progress*."

"You'll never get away with it. What about the authorities?"

"We have been doing this for thousands of years, and we have powerful forces on our side. Anyway, my proposal includes me calling off my forces for a while. And we could care less about your dad. Taking him out will just be a means to achieving our ultimate end—stopping you from saving souls. But, if we can come to terms, I'll spare him for now, too."

Stan and I were watching from the boardwalk bridge and I turned to him. "How comforting."

"They have not reached a deal yet," Stan pointed out.

"I will agree to give you one year. You do not need to quit entirely, although you are certainly free to do so. We're convinced you are saved, so we want to spare you for now. But we need you to at least stop, or slow down, your saving of other souls. Again, you do not need to stop totally, but you need to limit the number of souls you save. You can save yourself, of course, and Shelly. Good luck with that by the way."

"Further, Jak, you cannot minister through social media, or do any televangelism. You can continue to serve your church, but our research shows you are growing too fast. So over the next year your church membership cannot exceed one thousand members. That gives you some room to grow, but our downside is capped. And I want to see a formal amendment to your By-laws and Constitution capping your membership. I'm sure your dad can do that for you. If over the next year you violate any of this, all bets are off and we will immediately resume our tormenting and torture of you, your family, friends, and followers. But if you comply, we will leave you alone."

Jak had heard some of this before so he simply let Natas continue.

"But here is your real challenge, Jak," Natas would challenge Jak to a seemingly impossible task. "You need to try to save me, save my soul. If you do, we will leave you alone beyond the one-year period, or at least I can commit to you that I would no longer try to un-save anyone or spread anymore sin attractants. Furthermore, if you save me, all limits on your calling and ministry will be lifted, and you can save all you want."

Natas paused and appeared proud of his plan.

"And if I don't save you?"

"If you don't save me within a year, you can't save anyone anymore. You must voluntarily quit, or we will make sure you do. Do we have a deal, Jak?"

Jak studied Natas and sported a great poker face. He paused as if pondering the proposal. Then he revealed his cards.

"We have a deal, Natas."

"Good, and good luck with me, Jak. I'll be in touch."

When he stood up to leave, the dark arm from above again descended toward Natas. This time the hand touched Natas and then the hand and cloud slowly dissipated and disappeared.

As he walked away he turned back to Jak. Natas nodded and turned back to face Jak. "I was informed that, notwithstanding our deal, my leader has ordered me to carry out a piece of our original plan." He smiled a bit. "It's going to hurt Jak. I mean really hurt."

"Are you going to harm anyone who is saved?"

"Let me put it this way—we will not intentionally kill anyone who we believe is saved." That made Jak feel a little safer, but not much. He did not say anything and he had no idea what Natas had in mind.

"Sorry, Jak".

"Are you really?"

Natas shrugged. "What do you think?" He turned away without shaking Jak's hand and slowly left the park seeming to float away. Jak began his walk towards us.

I needed to check on the boys, so I dialed Jakob.

"Hello?"

My iPhone had scrambled his Caller ID, but his one-word sounded frightened. Stan also listened as I was on speaker.

"Jakob, it's Dad, are you guys okay?"

"Yeah, we're on the way home, but damn Dad, have you ever had someone point a loaded gun at you?"

I looked at Stan, "Actually, I have."

"Well, this gunman's eyes were cold and purposeful, and left no doubt his finger was willing. Dad, they almost had to do nothing because J-Rod and I were both practically scared to death anyway."

"I'm sorry."

"Well Dad, how do we avoid future confrontations with evil?"

"You're driving, Son. Let's discuss this tonight when I get home, but I am not sure we can."

Sheryl and the boys would be fine, for now.

Jak took his time as he was walking to join us on the boardwalk, probably wondering what in the world he just agreed to.

"Good job, Jak, but I don't know about this guy."

"I don't know either, Dad. I don't trust him, and I doubt I can save him."

"Guys, that guy is full of shit" Stan cautioned with incredible accuracy. "He is going to strike again, soon and Jak did you see...."

I quickly interrupted him. "It is worse than that, Stan—the man is actually full of evil." I did not know yet how or when to explain to Jak Natas's entrance into the park and the dark cloud and hand above them.

Dan joined us.

"Dan, I want you to work with Waster to come up with a plan to actually kidnap Natas's daughter this time. We need to be ready to strike back. Jak, you need to plan on at least making it look like you are trying to save him. But that is not happening. We might not even get to that point, as I suspect he is going to double-cross you as soon as possible."

Dan headed to his truck and said he was calling Waster to plan the kidnapping. We headed back to Jak's. During the drive Jak sensed a feeling of loss, a surreal uneasiness, unsure of its cause or causes. He missed Shelly, so he called her. She did not answer.

Natas had waited ten seconds after he assured himself of Sam's safety before he double-crossed Jak, and ordered his two thugs in Omaha back into action. Tin Man, and his sidekick Chubby, were back on a mission as soon as they released Jak's brothers and Natas believed Sam was freed. Abducting Shelly was easy because she exited the coffee shop the back way and into the alley. Why? No one will ever know. Maybe someone, or something, caused her to somehow betray Jak, too.

This time, instead of Omaha Steaks and Saul's Jewelry & Loan, instead of at an airport kiosk and a local pawnshop, Tin Man and Chubby obtained their tools at a simple Walgreens. Tin Man appeared abruptly from behind the dumpster and surprised her, scaring the hell out of her. But the fear did not last long as the chloroform-laced towel Tin Man smothered her face with quickly took hold with its intended effect. They threw her limp body in the back of the rental and left the alley. They would finish the task remotely. No witness would rat on them, for there was not even a rat to witness them.

Jak had left Shelly a voicemail, but she never got his message. She, of all people, the pastor's wife, never got Jak's message. He left her another one, and another. She never got any of his messages.

Jak did not know it yet, but at the tender young age of twenty-two, he had become a widower. He would never, ever see her again.

†

We made it back to Jak's and Goldie joined us on the porch. We talked about needing a brand new plan, but made little progress.

Stan was getting ready to leave, and said he was going to call Detective Crow as we promised.

"So you're going to give a full confession about Gil Egan's death?"

"I don't know, Rob. You got my back if I do?"

"I don't know."

"If I tell them I killed Egan because he was going to kill you, can you corroborate my story that Gil pulled his gun on me first?"

"You said you had reliable info that Egan was going to kill me so you intervened, but did you have to kill him?" I pushed back.

"I was going to try to reason with him, but he aimed his Beretta at me, didn't you see that?"

"I was watching through my rearview mirror." Which is where I wished all this was. "So everything was kind of backward, but even through two windshields I did see Egan flash something." I was coming around.

"If you can testify that you saw Egan flash or point something my way that will be enough. I know the strength of the prosecution we'll be up against and I can beat any charges they might bring. Besides, I have a feeling Jak's going to need my help further going forward, so I need your help to stay out of prison."

"You're right, Stan. I got your back. But call me right after you talk to Crow so we can go over what you discussed. We need to be fully aligned and on the same page, and I want to hear what was discussed from you, not the reporter."

"Got it."

Jak and I both gave Stan our sincere and heart-felt appreciation.

"And congrats again on your baptism Stan, that's great," I told him.

"And make sure you sustain it," added Jak, grinning of course.

I placed a hand on Stan's shoulder and shook his hand. "We don't always do the right thing, but stay saved my friend."

"I'll be in touch, Rob, and I'll see you Sunday, Jak." He drove off in Dan's Jag, safe and secure.

Given what I now had in mind to fight Natas back with, all three of our souls might be at risk. Jak's full potential would be tested.

Jak and I were still on the porch with Goldie.

"So Dad, when are you heading home?"

"In a few minutes actually, a broker is coming to pick me up."

"Broker? For what?"

"She's going to show me a few houses around here and then take me to the airport to fly home."

"Houses?"

"Yeah, I'm slowly losing my edge, the drive, I feel like I'm being left behind in some ways. So, I'm thinking of retiring or at least slowing down."

"But you're not that old, and can you, I mean, financially?"

"I've done well, and Mom and I have lived below our means for over two and a half decades. We've, for the most part, resisted the temptations to buy bigger and better houses, cars, toys, clothes, and other material things. Heck Jak, I don't even buy myself new clothes. When I need something I let Mom or others know before Christmas, my birthday, or Father's Day. And get this, I have not bought myself any tennis shoes for years. Ever since you boys got big enough that I could wear yours, when you thought yours were old and did not have any good miles left on them, and you tried to give them to Goodwill, I would take your hand-me-ups and wear them."

"Wow, Dad. I guess I never realized."

"There's many things about people close to us, ones we love, that we don't realize, appreciate, understand, or even know about. But I think that's human nature, son. Anyhow, I could probably not work another day in my life, but that would not be productive, or service to others. I think I can still help people—professionally, personally, and financially. I, of course, want to help you kids all I can."

"And we appreciate it, Dad."

"When you consistently spend less than you make over time and live below your means, the excess adds up. Mom and I have both spent and invested conservatively resulting in a nice nest egg. Besides, we'd keep our Omaha home and real estate interests, but maybe go ahead and get a place down here. I suspect it is a buyer's market, and there should be some good deals out there. I told the broker I'd like to see some properties on a lake or river, and then Mom and I can come back down again in a couple weeks to do some more looking."

"Cool, Dad."

I did not share with Jak, but I figured I would need to be here to help with Natas, anyway.

"Yeah, I kinda like it down here. We would not do anything permanent until J'Nay is out of high school, but we could get a place we could stay at when we visit. Maybe in a couple years I can work part-time out of our Atlanta office if I want to, and our main residence would be down here. Mom and I both think we might want to close out our time here on Earth with our son also being our pastor. We will have known our pastor all his life. Besides, we still have work to do, Son. We are only saved for now."

"Dad?"

"What?"

"I love you very much."

"I know, and I love you, too, and it's nice to say so once in a while but isn't it also nice to know when it goes without saying," I said more as a statement than a question.

A nice, silver Cadillac Seville drove up, a typical realtor's car. The woman started to approach the porch but I motioned her to stay. I grabbed my bag and briefcase, petted Goldie one more time, and gave her that last piece of pizza crust that I put on a porch window ledge. She missed me already. I received a big, strong hug from Jak, as he was unable to fight back a tear. He looked toward the heavens.

"Thank you, God, and I so love you."

"Bye, Dad, and thank you, literally, for everything." Jak's innocence had betrayed him. He had no idea.

Despite the tear, he grinned.

EPILOGUE

†

Four days later.

It was the saddest day of my life, so far.

His, too.

For many, perhaps most, the saddest day will be Judgment Day.

But the saddest day so far for us was today.

Her funeral was today.

Jak's first funeral as a pastor was for his wife. Somehow, the kid performed the funeral service at our church, the church they grew up in. Later, late that night, it was Jak and me out on our porch.

"I'm so sorry, son." I was barely able to tell him again. I had never hated someone, something so much. I wanted to kill Natas. Jak's red eyes had already cried a river, but his tears had slowed to resemble a couple of dripping faucets. His sobbing had subsided substantially. I had never felt such pain and sorrow for a living person. Or a dead one, for that matter. Then he started shouting his grief.

"Shelly come back, you can blame it all on me. Father, how could you …?"

He was yelling at God, and questioning Him.

I held him best I could but he was shaking so.

"I don't know what to say." I really didn't, but I was in despair myself.

God's hand seemed to comfort Jak a little and it may have grazed me as I managed some words.

"Though we walk in the valley of the shadow of death."

"Dad... I" He choked. "I still don't...think I'm going to quit. But God damn it," he wiped his eyes. "What the hell are we gonna do?"

He was weeping and wobbling.

"I don't know, son. Not yet anyway. But I already talked to Stan and Dan, and we agreed it's time to take our gloves off and fight back."

"Nooooo," he pled. "I need to get back to Atlanta."

"I know we do."

ACKNOWLEDGMENTS

I could not have written this book without the divine guidance from God and His Son. They were with me all the way and I could feel it. To Jesus and God go the Glory.

I am also greatly grateful for my Pastors. Thank you Pastor Scott Ross for marrying Cheryl and me over 2.5 decades ago, and for helping us keep our faith ever since. Thank you for helping keep all of us on the path. You baptized Cheryl, me and all our kids and have been there for us in lightness and dark. I am so happy for you and Gayle enjoying your retirement, just two houses down from us.

Additional appreciation is due my current Pastors—Pastor Scott Millard and our Associate Pastor Christy Ross Wibel. You continue to minister me and our family so wonderfully that we cannot thank you enough. Your messages, ministry and movements gave me more ideas and inspiration for this book than you'll ever know. Thank you for help with some of my religious questions and directing me to certain scriptures. I am sure you did not even know you were helping me sometimes—with this book, I mean.

I also acknowledge and thank Elaine Seier, who did most of the typing and correcting. She also really has helped me serve my clients as the best secretary I ever had during a 27-year law practice. And she really does bake us cinnamon rolls to fight for!

A big thanks goes to my publishing and editing team, led by Lisa Pelto, owner of Concierge Marketing. They helped me with all aspects of publishing, marketing, cover design and the book's layout. I also appreciated the professional work of my editor, Stacey Kucharik. Thank you Stacey for your corrections and suggestions.

My wife of almost 30 years, Cheryl, basically gave me my space and stayed out of the way. She knows me very well. But her intermittent inquiries gave me more energy.

Our four kids were my biggest inspiration. Suffice it to say, if my God loves me like I love my children, my God, does my God love me. Not sure though, that I could sacrifice one of mine like He did His only one, for me and you.

Finally, further acknowledgment goes to two of my best friends, Itty Bitty and Teddy. They spent many writing sessions with me, sometimes out with me in a lawn chair, or curled up by my side down in our man and dog cave. Their parts in this book are non-fiction, and they are the only "characters" who retain their real name from real life.

www.ingramcontent.com/pod-product-compliance
Lightning Source LLC
Chambersburg PA
CBHW020641260626
47157CB00008B/2853